SPECIAL MESSAGE TO READERS

This book is published by
THE ULVERSCROFT FOUNDATION
a registered charity in the U.K., No. 264873

The Foundation was established in 1974 to provide funds to help towards research, diagnosis and treatment of eye diseases. Below are a few examples of contributions made by
THE ULVERSCROFT FOUNDATION:

A new Children's Assessment Unit
at Moorfield's Hospital, London.
•
Twin operating theatres at the
Western Ophthalmic Hospital, London.
•
The Frederick Thorpe Ulverscroft Chair of
Ophthalmology at the University of Leicester.
•
Eye Laser equipment to various eye hospitals.

If you would like to help further the work of the Foundation by making a donation or leaving a legacy, every contribution, no matter how small, is received with gratitude. Please write for details to:

**THE ULVERSCROFT FOUNDATION,
The Green, Bradgate Road, Anstey,
Leicester LE7 7FU. England
Telephone: (0533)364325**

COYOTE WINTER

Major Joe Daly and his gang of cold-blooded killers, nicknamed the Wyoming Phantoms, carry out a series of stagecoach hold-ups. To ensure that nobody can identify them, they murder all their victims. When they make a mistake and Amy Scarlett, a former saloon-girl, survives one of their hold-ups, they determine to track her down and kill her. However, they reckon without the intervention of the dangerous and deadly Kentuckian gunfighter, Jack Stone.

*Books by J. D. Kincaid
in the Linford Western Library:*

CORRIGAN'S REVENGE
THE FOURTH OF JULY
SHOWDOWN AT MEDICINE CREEK

J. D. KINCAID

COYOTE WINTER

Complete and Unabridged

LINFORD
Leicester

First published in Great Britain in 1991 by
Robert Hale Limited
London

First Linford Edition
published November 1993
by arrangement with
Robert Hale Limited
London

The right of J. D. Kincaid to be identified as
the author of this work has been asserted by
him in accordance with the
Copyright, Designs and Patents Act, 1988

Copyright © 1991 by J. D. Kincaid
All rights reserved

British Library CIP Data

Kincaid, J. D.
 Coyote winter.—Large print ed.—
Linford western library
I. Title II. Series
823.914 [F]

ISBN 0–7089–7442–2

Published by
F. A. Thorpe (Publishing) Ltd.
Anstey, Leicestershire

Set by Words & Graphics Ltd.
Anstey, Leicestershire
Printed and bound in Great Britain by
T. J. Press (Padstow) Ltd., Padstow, Cornwall

This book is printed on acid-free paper

To Tom and Yvonne

1

A CHILL wind blew straight off the Wyoming prairie and through the town. It was a bleak, below zero January and the snow lay deep on the ground. Jack Stone stirred and slowly awakened. The hotel bedroom was as cold as charity, with the window panes frosted on both the inside and the outside. Buffalo in midwinter was no place to be, Stone reckoned. The trouble was, he was there and ahead of him he had a goddam long ride south to Texas. To get to where he was going, he would have to leave snowbound Wyoming, then travel the entire length of Colorado and a fair distance across New Mexico. Stone smiled wryly. He had till the spring to make it. Hal Roberts wasn't expecting him till then. Hal didn't need him till then. Maybe he would stop off in Denver and Albuquerque on his way down south? A feller could have himself some fun in those two towns.

Stone glanced at the girl in bed beside him. Small and petite, and with those oh-so-innocent blue eyes, the redhead could easily have been mistaken for some demure young virgin, but that she most certainly was not. She had been the best-looking of the Golden Nugget's girls, and Stone hadn't had a woman in a long, long while. Well, he had made up for lost time, for they had sure enjoyed one helluva night together. Stone reckoned she was about the sexiest, randiest little wild-cat he had bedded in years. Consequently, he had had little or no sleep, which probably accounted for the fact that he felt so darned weary.

The girl opened one eye and peered at him. She grinned wickedly.

"That was some night!" she sighed.

"Sure was, Sandy," replied Stone.

"You don't believe in givin' a girl no rest, do you?" she chuckled.

"Not when she's as temptin' a dish as you."

"Hmm. A compliment. That's nice."

Sandy smiled warmly at the big man. She had, in her young life, shared many a bed with many a man. But tonight had been special. She carefully scanned his craggy, square-cut features, observing the grey-flecked brown hair, the cool blue eyes and the broken nose. He had been handsome once, she thought. Still was when he smiled, which he did but rarely. Sandy wondered why the night had been so special. She couldn't explain it, but there had been a certain rapport between them, not something she experienced with many of her customers.

She knew, of course, that Stone was the legendary Kentuckian gunfighter who had tamed Mallory, Colorado's roughest, toughest mining town. His body bore the scars of many a gunfight, for he had fought in the Civil War, and only survived the violent years that followed it by dint of his speed and accuracy with a gun, his quick wits and his matchless courage. Stone had grown up fast since he was orphaned at fourteen. He had suffered more than his share of tragedy in his thirty-odd years. The mental scars were not visible, but they were just as real as those which marked his muscular, two hundred pound frame. They had made him what he was.

"I was plannin' on lammin' outta town today," growled the Kentuckian, gazing ruefully at the frosted window.

"You in a tearin' hurry to leave Buffalo?" asked the girl.

"Nope. Guess not."

"Then, stay over another day."

"Yeah. Why not?" Stone grinned and, turning, began to stroke one of the girl's smooth white shoulders. "Never do today what you can put off till tomorrow, huh?" he said.

"That's right."

Sandy took Stone's head between her hands and pressed her soft red lips to his. Stone felt her small, firm breasts thrust hard against his chest. His arms went round her slender body, one hand encompassing her narrow waist and the other clasping her neatly-rounded bottom.

"Mmm, that's nice!" murmured the girl between kisses.

"Sure is," replied the Kentuckian.

He rolled over on top of her. As he did so, a stream of icy-cold air was admitted beneath the blankets, causing both of them to gasp. Such was the fury of their lovemaking, however, they soon warmed up again. While the winter wind howled outside the hotel and the temperature inside remained below zero, Stone and the girl were cocooned in a little world of their own: warm, cosy and intimate. It was a world that both were reluctant to contemplate leaving.

★ ★ ★

It was late on the following morning when Jack Stone eventually quit his bed. He dressed hurriedly while Sandy watched him from beneath the blankets. He pulled on a faded grey shirt, well-worn denim pants and much travelled boots. Then he tied a red kerchief round his thick, strong neck. Next he strapped on his Frontier Model Colt, tying the holster down to his right thigh. Finally, he pulled on his knee-length buckskin jacket, slapped on his grey Stetson and picked up his Winchester from the corner of the bedroom, where it had stood propped against the closet.

"That all yo're wearin'?" exclaimed Sandy. "Hell, you ride out like that an' you'll freeze to death!"

Stone grinned.

"I got me a sheepskin coat lashed to my bedroll," he replied. "I left 'em together with my saddle over at the livery stables."

"Wa'al, I hope they're all still there."

"They will be."

Sandy looked quizzically at the big Kentuckian.

"You got more faith in human nature than I have," she said.

"Human nature ain't got nothin' to do with it," drawled Stone.

"No?"

"Nope. I asked Art Chaney to take care of 'em for me."

"Wa'al, Art ain't exactly Buffalo's most trustworthy citizen, Jack. He could always say the coat an' the saddle had been stolen, an' then . . ."

"He won't."

Sandy stared into Stone's ice-cold blue eyes. He had been plumb easy-going and good-natured in his dealings with her, but the look in those eyes made her suddenly realise that the Kentuckian was not a man to cross. If Art Chaney had any sense at all, he would have taken very good care of the items entrusted to him by Stone.

The redhead sat up in bed, her small, firm breasts bouncing up and down before Stone's appreciative gaze.

"You certain you don't wanta stay over a while longer?" she asked seductively. Stone shook his head.

"Nope. I gotta long ways to go. Guess it's time to move on."

"Wa'al, it's sure been fun, Jack. An', if ever yo're this way again . . . " She left the rest unsaid, but the invitation was clear.

"I'll look you up," grinned Stone. You can bet on that."

He left the girl snuggling down once more beneath the blankets and made his way downstairs. The bar-room was practically deserted. He crossed the floor and pushed his way out through the batwing doors.

As he emerged from the Golden Nugget, Stone observed a small crowd had gathered outside the stage line depot. They stood round watching as the Wells Fargo stagecoach was loaded up. Stone strolled across towards the stage, for he had to pass the depot to reach Art Chaney's livery stables.

He watched the passengers clamber

aboard. All were wrapped up warmly against the bitter winter weather. There were two elderly gentlemen in frock-coats with fur collars, both of whom were wearing stove-pipe hats and carrying blankets to wrap round their legs. They were directors of the Cattlemen's Bank, on their way to confer with the board of the West and Frontier Bank in Laramie about a possible merger. A tall, thin, cheroot-smoking man in a Derby hat and ankle-length leather coat was the next to board the stage. He was a Pinkerton man, employed by Wells Fargo to investigate a recent spate of hold-ups. And he was followed by a short, tubby, red-faced whiskey salesman, swathed in blankets and a fur coat, clutching a carpet-bag and sporting a trapper's raccoon-skin hat with ear-flaps. The fifth and final passenger was a woman. Her blonde hair, although once natural, now owed some of its blondeness to a bottle; she was in her late thirties, but had certainly worn well. Apart from a few lines round the eyes and mouth, her pretty, oval face remained remarkably youthful. Her bright blue eyes twinkled provocatively and her figure was full, firm and voluptuous. Riper than it had been in her prime, it was nevertheless still good enough to excite the passions of any normal, red-blooded male. The woman wore a dark-red, figure-clinging gown and matching bonnet, with a cape of the same colour and material draped over her slender shoulders.

As Stone stepped up onto the sidewalk beside the stage, he was arrested by a voice calling his name. He turned to find himself face-to-face with the shotgun guard, a stocky, broad-shouldered man in a sheepskin coat and low-crowned black Stetson. The man was of approximately the same age as Stone and had a craggy, weatherbeaten face framed by a square-cut, grey-streaked beard. It was the beard that foxed Stone at first. Then, suddenly, he recognised the man. Bart Newton! Stone grinned. Bart Newton had been a fresh-faced young trooper when last they had met. They had fought together on the Union side throughout the five years of the Civil War.

"Jeeze, Bart Newton! How are you, you ole hound-dog?" asked Stone.

"Fine, Jack, jest fine. But, what in tarnation, are you doin' up here? Last time I heard, you was down Kansas way, helpin' Wild Bill Hickok clean up Abilene."

"Yeah. Wa'al, I got me outta that kinda work some years back."

"But, why, Jack? Hell, you was allus darned good with a gun!"

"Too good, mebbe."

"Whaddya mean?"

"I mean, I got myself one helluva reputation."

"Sure did. Yo're a livin' legend, Jack."

"Which is why I quit gun-fightin'."

"Yo're still wearin' a gun, though."

"For my own protection, Bart. But, these days, I do my level best to avoid trouble. As a law officer, I was all the time attractin' cocky young gunslingers out to make a reputation for theirselves by gunnin' me down. Instead of scarin' off troublemakers, I was bringin' 'em in. Not what folks expected of their sheriff."

"Guess not. So, what are you doin' to earn an honest buck?"

"Mainly ranch work, or mebbe ridin' herd on the big cattle drives. I don't stay no place long." Stone grinned wryly and added, "At present, I'm headin' south to Texas, where, come the spring, I figure on doin' a li'l bronco-bustin' for an ole buddy of ours, Hal Roberts."

"Cap'n Hal Roberts?"

"The same."

"Wa'al, dang my hide! He was jest a kid when we knew him. A reg'lar greenhorn."

"Now he has a ten thousand acre spread close to San Antonio."

"Whew!"

"Like to ride along, Bart? As I recall, you were no slouch when it came to breakin' in hosses."

"No thanks, Jack. I'm a darned sight too old for that kinda game."

"Yo're no older than me."

"Even so." Newton laughed and shook his head. "I'll stick to what I'm doin'," he said.

"Ridin' shotgun for Wells Fargo?"

"You got it."

"Darned cold work in midwinter."

Bart Newton pulled the collar of his coat close round his neck and screwed up his eyes against the biting wind that blew down Main Street.

"Yup, it sure is," he growled.

"A man could freeze to death sittin' on the box of a stage," commented Stone.

"I ain't comin' with you, Jack, so quit tryin' to persuade me," replied the guard. "But yo're goddam right, this freezin' winter weather is fit only for coyotes, wolves an' bears. It sure ain't fit for human bein's."

"At least it ain't gonna encourage no bandits to sit around out there on the plains waitin' for you."

"Don't you believe it. There've been no fewer than three stages held up in these parts over the last coupla months."

"Holy cow! Ain't Wells Fargo doin' nothin' about it?"

"Yeah. They've sent up half-a-dozen of their own agents, an' engaged some Pinkerton men, too." Newton jerked a thumb over his left shoulder in the direction of the stagecoach. "See that thin feller in the brown leather coat an' the derby hat?" he whispered.

Stone glanced in through the window at the thin man, who was sitting back in his seat and smoking his cheroot.

"I see him," he growled.

"He's a Pinkerton man. He's gonna start his investigations at Casper. His pardner got out here," said the guard.

"Wa'al, them Pinkerton fellers are s'posed to be pretty darned good. Guess they'll soon git on to the trail of the bandits who've been holdin' up the stages," drawled Stone.

"I ain't so sure," said Newton. Y'see, nobody knows what the bandits look like."

"Whaddya mean? Surely some of the victims . . . "

"None of 'em has survived. At each of the three hold-ups, the murderin' bastards have gunned down every last one of 'em."

"Jeeze!"

"Men, women an' even children. Which is why Wells Fargo reckon it's the same gang that's responsible for all three hold-ups. Newspapers have dubbed 'em the Wyomin' Phantoms."

Stone frowned. He held no truck for any kind of outlaw. But the kind that could gun down defenceless women and children, they made him madder than a grizzly with its paw in a trap.

"You take care, then, Bart," he said solemnly.

"Sure thing." Newton clapped the barrel of his shotgun. "They try holdin' up this here stage an' I'll blast the livin' daylights outta them!"

Stone smiled grimly.

"You said yo're headin' for Casper?" he said.

"That's right. The stage is bound for Casper and then on to Laramie."

"Wa'al, I'm headin' south myself, an' I planned to pass through both them towns," said Stone.

"So, ride along with us, Jack."

The Kentuckian thought for a moment.

"When are you startin' out?" he asked.

Bart Newton glanced up at the driver on the box.

"We ready, Jesse?" he called.

"Jest as soon as you git up here, Bart," replied the driver.

"We're startin' out right now," said Newton, turning to Stone.

"Then, guess I'll have to catch you up later, for I figure to git myself some breakfast 'fore I ride out," drawled the Kentuckian.

"A wise move, Jack."

The guard held out a large, horny

hand. Stone grasped it and the two men embraced.

"You should overhaul us sometime 'fore we reach the stagin'-post at Bighorn Springs. We'll have ourselves a few drinks there, an' chew over old times," said Newton.

"You bet," replied Stone.

"Be seein' you."

"Yup."

The guard smiled at Stone and then clambered up onto the box beside the driver.

"Okay, Jesse, let's git goin'," he rasped.

The driver grinned broadly, then let out a whoop and, cracking his whip and flicking his reins, set the stagecoach rattling through the town and out on to the snow-covered trail.

Stone watched it go and then proceeded on his way to Art Chaney's livery stables. He looked in and told Chaney to have his bay gelding ready and saddled within the hour. That done, he continued along the sidewalk until he reached Ma Campbell's establishment.

In Buffalo a man could get a woman, a drink and a bed at the Golden Nugget, but, if he wanted something to eat, he moseyed on over to Ma Campbell's place. Stone paused in front of the door and glanced up at the sign immediately above it.

'Mrs Miriam Campbell's High-Class Eating-House,' it read, and, stuck to the window, were two large notices. One informed the public that, 'You Can Eat As Much As You Like For One Dollar', while the other proclaimed, 'No Alcohol. No Spitting. No Swearing. No Shooting. By Order Of the Proprietress'.

Stone grinned and went in.

2

THE five men crouched down among the boulders on the top of the ridge. The boulders offered some protection from the icy wind whistling across the prairie, but not much. From their vantage point, the five could see many miles both north and south along the trail.

Joe Daly scoured it with the same binoculars he had used during his time as an officer of the Confederate Army. He still found it hard to come to terms with the South's defeat and the changes which that defeat had brought. He had lost everything he held dear: his young wife, his family, his home. And this had left him a deeply embittered man. After the war he had ridden with Quantrell's raiders, and then he had gone his own way, although continuing to live by the gun.

It was in Providence Flats that Daly had met the others. Providence Flats was a town beyond the law. There was no sheriff. The town existed solely to provide for the needs of men like Daly, the scum of the earth: outlaws, gamblers and renegades. Four saloons, six bordellos, one hotel, one general store and some livery stables. That was Providence Flats.

Joe Daly was a big man. Big, blond and handsome. He was also an educated man, and a man without scruples. He still wore his Confederate officer's uniform, although he had cut off all the army insignia. Nonetheless, he insisted that the others refer to him as 'Major'. A sabre scar decorated his left cheek, a souvenir of Gettysburg. He shivered inside his greatcoat and turned to survey the other members of his gang.

They were a rough, tough bunch, hardened killers each and every one of them. But none had complained when Daly had laid down the rules by which they were to operate. As leader, Daly expected the others to obey his orders without question. And, so that they would never find their names and faces on any 'Wanted' poster, he had decreed that there were to be no survivors among their victims. They would shoot down all of them: driver, guard and passengers. This they had done without compunction on the three stagecoach robberies they had so far committed. One more hold-up and they could rest up for a while. Maybe spend the remainder of the winter drinking, gambling and whoring in Providence Flats?

The one-time Confederate officer had chosen his gang carefully. The brothers, Elmer and Eli Judd, were men after his own heart: cold, merciless killers who respected neither man nor beast. Elmer was four years older than Eli, yet, with their heavy beards and weatherbeaten faces, they could have been mistaken for twins. Both sported battered grey Stetsons and ankle-length sheepskin coats, and they were similarly armed, each carrying a Remington in his holster and a .30 calibre Spencer rifle in his saddleboot.

Where the brothers were both squat and gnome-like, Bear was a mountain of a man. Nobody knew him by any name other than Bear. And the name suited him. A ruddy, pockmarked face peered out from behind black bushy whiskers and a black bushy beard, and the giant was dressed in a beaver hat and a huge bearskin coat. At a distance he could easily have been mistaken for a grizzly. Like the brothers, he carried a Remington in his holster. He also had a huge, razor-sharp Bowie knife in a sheath at his waist and in his saddleboot there was a long-barrelled buffalo-gun, a Sharps rifle with telescopic sights, which was amazingly accurate up to a distance of approximately three-quarters of a mile.

The fifth member of the gang was a nineteen-year-old youth. But, despite his tender years, Randy Wilkins had already killed no fewer than a dozen men, two women and one five-year-old child. He was as crazy as could be and as dangerous as a copperhead. His hero was the late, unlamented Billy the Kid, and he dressed all in black, even to the extent of wearing a long black leather coat over his black shirt and levis. A matched pair of .45 calibre, pearl-handled British Tranters sat neatly in Wilkins' two holsters, while a Winchester was jammed firmly into his saddleboot. Small, thin, narrow-shouldered and with a pinched, sickly-white face, Randy Wilkins would have been hard pressed to beat a sturdy thirteen-year-old in a fist-fight. But, then, he did not fight with his fists. Gun-fights were more his métier.

"Wa'al, Major, any sight of the stage yet?" he enquired in a thin, reedy voice.

Joe Daly lifted his binoculars and peered anxiously across the snow-white prairie. The trail snaked northwards towards Buffalo. For the moment it was deserted.

"Nope; nothin'," growled Daly.

"Hell, we hang on here much longer an' we'll freeze to death!" the youth complained.

"If 'n' you wanta lam outta here, Randy, yo're welcome to do jest that," drawled Daly. "I reckon me an' the rest of the boys can take the stage when it comes. An' I sure ain't averse to splittin' the spoils four ways instead of five."

"I'll bet you ain't," said Wilkins. He peered out from beneath the wide brim of his low-crowned black Stetson, his cold grey eyes glittering wickedly. "Guess I'll hang on. I didn't come all this way jest for the ride," he muttered.

Daly nodded and, turning abruptly, resumed his gaze northwards along the trail. The glare from the snow did not help. He squinted awkwardly. Then, all at once, he saw it. First of all, he noticed the snow-clouds kicked up by the horses' hooves. A few seconds later, he recognised the distant black speck on the horizon that was the stagecoach. And eventually he found that he could pick out the stage and the horses separately and quite distinctly.

"Okay, Bear, go git that there rifle of youm," he rasped.

The giant outlaw grinned broadly, revealing an ugly set of decaying, blackening teeth. He lumbered off towards the horses, which were tethered below the ridge and out of sight of the trail. Upon reaching his roan, Bear pulled the long-barrelled Sharps rifle clear of the saddleboot. Then, grasping the gun, he hurried back up the slope to the top of the ridge. He crouched down beside Daly.

"Time to use ole Betsy, huh?" he grunted, slapping the stock of his rifle with a huge hand.

"Yeah. You know what you gotta do?" muttered Daly.

"I oughta by now."

"Then do it!"

Bear rested the Sharps' long barrel on top of the boulder in front of him and began to focus on the still distant, yet fast-moving stagecoach. An evil leer split his ugly, heavily bearded face as he took careful aim at the stagecoach driver.

"Who'll I pick off first, Major?" he asked.

"The feller ridin' shotgun," replied Daly.

"Yessir."

Bear adjusted his aim slightly. Now it was the shotgun guard's features which were sharply in focus. Bear slowly curled his finger round the trigger of the Sharps rifle.

★ ★ ★

Inside the stagecoach four of the five passengers were shivering. Neither their heavy clothing, nor the blankets some of them had draped over themselves, seemed sufficient to completely blot out the bitter cold. And the view from the stage's windows did not help matters. All they could see was mile upon mile of Wyoming's snowy wasteland.

The one person who was not feeling the cold was Harry Platt, the whiskey salesman. His raccoon-skin hat and fur coat kept him snug as a bug in a rug. Also, prior to setting out, he had taken the precaution of consuming half a bottle of his merchandise.

"You folks look to be sufferin' pretty badly from the cold," he remarked cheerfully.

"We sure ain't sufferin' from the heat," replied the Pinkerton man laconically.

"Wa'al, sir, let me offer you a slug of Carson's Three Star Rye Whiskey, the smoothest an' the best yo're ever likely to taste. It'll warm you up some," said Platt.

So saying, the salesman opened his carpet-bag and, from among an array of full bottles, produced the bottle he had already started. He removed the top and handed the bottle to the Pinkerton man.

"Thank you, sir," said the Pinkerton

man, gladly taking hold of the bottle and gulping down a fair measure of the amber liquor.

"Would you gentlemen care for a slug?" enquired Platt, fixing a curious eye upon the two elderly passengers.

"Er . . . no, thank you," replied the taller of the two.

"No, thank you," added his companion.

They were sorely tempted, yet both considered it to be beneath their dignity to share a bottle with their fellow-passengers. After all, as directors of the Cattlemen's Bank, they were men of substance and position.

Harry Platt shrugged his shoulders and turned and smiled broadly at the blonde woman who was sitting opposite him.

"I guess I forgot my manners, ma'am," he said. "I should've offered you first slug, you bein' a lady."

The emphasis which Platt laid upon the word 'lady' told the blonde that he regarded her as anything but a lady. However, that did not worry her. Amy

Scarlett had suffered a great deal worse than innuendo in her thirty-seven years. Orphaned at five, she had in her time been beggar, drudge, thief and whore. Then, at the age of twenty-seven, she had teamed up with a certain Clancy O'Rourke, an Irish con-man and gambler with a silver tongue and a lucky streak. Together they had won sufficient funds to buy the Jack of Hearts Saloon in Sheridan. Ten years later, O'Rourke had taken up with a new lady-love, a twenty-year-old dancer called Mandy. But Amy had had the good sense to make her partnership in the Jack of Hearts Saloon both legal and binding. Consequently, O'Rourke had been forced to buy her out, and Amy had received a considerable sum of money from him. She had paid this into her bank account, which she had arranged to be transferred to the bank's branch in San Francisco. There she intended to start up in business on her own, and this time it was to be a respectable business, for Amy's ambition was to open a high-class dress shop. She was currently on her way to Laramie, where she planned to catch the transcontinental train to San Francisco.

"I don't reckon I'll have any of yore whiskey, thanks all the same," she said.

"You'll be tellin' us that a lady like you don't entertain drinkin' strong liquor," sneered Platt.

"I didn't say that."

"Nope. You didn't." Platt grinned and wagged a finger at the blonde. "You sure look respectable in yore smart noo gown an' bonnet, but I remember you when you was no better 'n you oughta be," he stated.

"Indeed?"

"Oh, yeah! Yo're Amy Scarlett, ain't you?"

"That's my name, yes."

"Wa'al, I recall you was peddlin' yore trade at the Lucky Strike in Denver when . . ."

"That was a long time ago."

"Once a whore, always a whore." Platt leaned forward and, breathing whiskey fumes into Amy's face, murmured lasciviously, "Mebbe you an' me could git together at the next stop-over an' have ourselves some fun, huh?"

Amy stared back at the whiskey salesman with ice-cold blue eyes and then, without saying a single word, slapped him hard across the face.

"Hell!" he exclaimed. "There wasn't no call for you to do that!"

"I don't care to be propositioned in public by no drunken lunkhead," replied Amy tartly. "Nor do I care to have my past raked over in front of total strangers."

"The lady's right," drawled the Pinkerton man. "You go tryin' to embarrass her in public, you deserve to have yore face slapped."

Platt turned angrily upon the detective.

"Who the hell d'you think you are to lecture me?" he rasped. "What happens 'tween me an' Miss Scarlett ain't no concern of yourn. 'Sides, considerin' you jest accepted a slug of my whiskey, I'd 've thought . . ."

"I'll pay you for it, if you like," replied the Pinkerton man contemptuously.

"Now, look here . . . " began Platt.

"No, you look here," snapped the other. "We got a long ways to go yet, an' I reckon, if 'n' we cain't behave decent to one another, it's gonna be one helluva long, uncomfortable ride."

"So, what are you sayin'?"

"I'm sayin', feller, that you best shuddup."

"I concur," said the taller of the two bankers.

"Yessir. It would be appreciated by us all if you would keep yore unseemly thoughts to yoreself," added the second banker.

Harry Platt glared furiously at the two men in their frock coats and stovepipe hats. Then, he took another slug from his whiskey bottle and pointedly turned and stared out of the window.

Amy smiled gratefully at the Pinkerton man.

"Thank you, Mr . . . er . . . ?"

"Holt. Jim Holt."

"You travellin' through to Laramie?" enquired Amy.

"Nope. I'm gittin' out at Casper. I got some business to attend to there."

"Wa'al, I'll be glad of yore company at least that far," said the blonde, and she glanced anxiously across the coach in the direction of the whiskey salesman.

Jim Holt smiled and promptly nudged his fellow-passenger in the ribs. Harry Platt started and, turning to face the Pinkerton man, scowled darkly.

"Where are you headin', mister?" asked Holt.

"I don't see that's none of yore darned business," replied Platt.

"I'm makin' it my business," said Holt.

Platt continued to scowl at the thin man, but, noting the icy glint in Holt's eye, he eventually shrugged his shoulders and muttered reluctantly, "Wa'al, if you must know, I'm aimin' to git out at Casper. Got me some business to transact there. Jest like yoreself."

Holt nodded. His eyes met Amy's and they both smiled. Holt slowly produced a fresh cheroot from a narrow tin case.

"That seems to be OK then, ma'am," he said to Amy. "Don't reckon you need worry 'bout . . ."

But he never finished what he had to say, for at that moment there was the sound of a distant shot and a nearby cry, and a body tumbled off the box and hurtled past the left-hand window of the stagecoach. Immediately, one of the two bankers poked his head out of the window and peered back along the trail.

"Holy cow!" he exclaimed. "That . . . that was our guard!"

"The feller ridin' shotgun?" demanded Holt.

"Yes. Why . . ."

But the banker, too, was interrupted. A second shot rang out and this time it was the driver who was hit. He hung onto the reins, slumping back on the box. The bullet had ripped through his rib-cage and penetrated one lung. Coughing up blood, he valiantly attempted to control the horses. They, however, had been panicked by the shots and were galloping hell-for-leather along the trail. The struggle was a hopeless one and was abruptly ended when a third slug from Bear's buffalo-gun struck the driver in the forehead, blasting blood and brains out through the back of his skull and toppling him from the stagecoach.

The stage rattled on at breakneck speed, drawn by the sweating, terrified horses. Inside, the passengers prepared for the worst.

"It's them Wyomin' Phantoms, I know it is!" cried an alarmed Harry Platt.

"What are you talking about?" demanded the shorter of the two bankers.

"I read about 'em in the *Buffalo*

Bugle," said Platt. "They . . . they're a bunch of cold-blooded killers!"

"Wa'al, here they come," said Jim Holt, peering out of the window. He was right. Joe Daly and his gang had mounted up and were galloping down from the ridge, their horses kicking up little spurts of snow as they descended towards the trail.

Holt pulled a Colt Peacemaker from beneath his ankle-length leather coat and took careful aim. He fired. But shooting from a fast-moving, jolting stage at an equally fast-moving horseman was no easy task, and he missed. He tried a second shot, and a third, and was just about to squeeze the trigger a fourth time when the bandits responded.

Joe Daly and both the Judd brothers fired simultaneously. Daly's shot buried itself in the side of the stage, six inches above Holt's head. Elmer Judd's bullet smashed through the framework of the door and lodged in the back of the seat, mid-way between the two bankers' heads. But Eli Judd's found its mark. It struck Jim Holt between the eyes and exploded inside his skull, shattering his brain and killing him instantly.

"Oh, my God!" screamed Amy Scarlett.

She turned chalk-white, while Harry Platt's ruddy complexion faded into a greenish-grey pallor.

"What . . . what shall we do?" cried the bankers in unison.

"Are either of you fellers carryin' a gun?" enquired Amy.

Both shook their heads. She turned to Harry Platt.

"What about you?" she demanded.

Platt pulled an ancient Navy Colt from the depths of his carpet-bag.

"I . . . I ain't never fired it," he confessed nervously. "Don't rightly know how."

"Wa'al, now's yore chance to learn," said the blonde, and she opened her reticule and withdrew a small but deadly-looking, two-barrelled Derringer. "Let's at least make a fight of it," she cried.

Platt looked doubtful.

"I . . . I dunno. Mebbe if we offer 'em no resistance, they'll spare our lives? Whaddya think?" he asked.

Amy laughed, but there was no humour in her laugh.

"If 'n' you was right earlier when you said they was the Wyomin' Phantoms, then they ain't gonna spare nobody's life. So, how's about goin' down fightin'?"

As Amy spoke, Joe Daly rode past on one side of the stage, while Elmer Judd peered in at the opposite window. Judd was clutching a Remington, which he aimed directly at Harry Platt.

"Drop that gun!" he roared.

The whiskey salesman promptly did as he was bid, throwing the Navy Colt back into the carpet-bag. But Amy was made of sterner stuff. She turned and fired at the outlaw. Owing to the uneven motion of the stagecoach, she missed and, before she could attempt a second shot, Judd had leapt from his saddle and dived in through the window and knocked the Derringer from her hand. As it hit the floor, the taller of the two bankers made a grab for it. He scooped up the gun and aimed it at the outlaw, who had fallen on top of the blonde and was struggling to free himself from her embrace. She, for her part, was attempting, somewhat optimistically, to wrestle him to the floor and relieve him of his Remington revolver.

The banker's finger had curled round the trigger and he was just about to shoot when Eli Judd rode up and glanced in through the window of the stagecoach. Observing that his brother was in imminent danger of being shot in the back, the outlaw straightway aimed and fired his Remington at the banker. He fired twice in rapid succession. The two slugs ploughed through the banker's body, one shattering his spine and the other ripping straight through flesh and muscle and exiting in a spurting stream of blood and shattered bone. The banker cried out, the gun in his hand tilted skywards and his shot, when it came, blasted harmlessly into the roof of the stage. He then toppled forwards, to land on top of the struggling couple.

At the same moment, the stagecoach came to a juddering halt, Joe Daly having succeeded in the meantime in mounting the box and grabbing hold of the reins. As he struggled to control and calm the panic-stricken horses and the coach swung back and forth on groaning springs, Eli Judd threw open one of its doors, while Randy Wilkins yanked open the other.

"Okay, you folks, git out!" yelled Eli Judd.

"Yeah. Double-quick, or I start shootin'!" added the black-clad youth in his thin, reedy voice.

The first to emerge from the stage-coach was the surviving banker. He tumbled out, just as Bear rode up on his roan. The giant outlaw, having been engaged in shooting both the driver and the shotgun guard, had been a little behind the others in mounting his horse. Consequently, he had been the last of the five desperadoes to ride down from the ridge. Bear reined in his horse beside Randy Wilkins' black mare and added his voice to the others'.

"That's right," he roared. "Shift yore goddam selves, 'fore I cut yore guts out!"

And he leered at them, flourishing his Bowie knife and grinning wickedly.

Harry Platt had no wish to be either shot or knifed. Therefore, he descended from the coach with great haste and little dignity, though still clutching his carpet-bag. The next to emerge was Elmer Judd. He dragged out the third and last survivor of the hold-up, a whey-faced and thoroughly dishevelled Amy Scarlett. But she, at least, was not giving up without a fight. She continued to struggle with the outlaw, gamely attempting to claw his face and kick him in the shins. Finally, he dealt her a savage backhanded blow to the side of her face, which knocked her to the ground.

"Goddam hell-cat!" he rasped, and he lashed out with his boot, catching the blonde hard in the ribs.

Amy screamed and doubled up. She clutched her side and lay there gasping, tears of intermingled pain and rage streaming down her face.

Joe Daly clambered down from the box, an Army Model Colt in his right hand. He glanced idly at the prostrate blonde, then grinned at Elmer Judd and turned his attention to the interior of the stagecoach. He climbed inside and satisfied himself that both Jim Holt and the banker were dead.

Thereupon, he descended onto the snow-covered trail and addressed the three survivors.

"The main aim of this raid," he explained, "was to git hold of the J. B. Boxleiter Meat Processin' Factory wages, which Wells Fargo is transportin' from the Cattlemen's Bank in Buffalo to the company office in Casper. But that don't mean we ain't interested in takin' yore personal valuables," he added.

"You ... you can have everythin' I've got!" cried Harry Platt eagerly, and he hurriedly emptied the contents of both his wallet and the carpet-bag onto the snow. The bitter wind whipped away the few bank-notes, while the bottles of whiskey clanked noisily together. "The f ... finest rye w ... whiskey you'll ever taste. C ... Carson's Three Star," stammered Platt.

Daly made no attempt to pursue the vanishing bank-notes. He did, however, bend down and pick up one of the bottles. He removed the cork and took a quick slug of the amber liquor.

"Hmm, this ain't at all bad," he murmured, as he passed the bottle on to Bear.

"Kinda warmin'," commented the blackbearded giant.

He handed the bottle to Eli Judd and, while it continued on its way round the outlaws, Joe Daly turned his attention to the surviving banker.

"You look to be a man who's worth a few dollars," he rasped.

"I . . . I am, sir," replied the banker nervously.

"Then, you can share yore good fortune with us," said Daly.

"Unfortunately, I . . . er . . . I am carrying very little cash with me, though you are welcome to what I have."

So saying, the banker pulled out his wallet and tossed it to the bandit chief. Daly caught it deftly and, having removed a thick wad of bank-notes, dropped it down beside Harry Platt's whiskey bottles. He studied the notes, observing that the majority were twenty-dollar bills.

"I wouldn't call this very little cash," he said, as he gleefully riffled through the notes. "But, then, I ain't rich like you, so I guess we don't see things quite the same."

"N . . . no. I guess not," said the banker.

"An' now, how's 'bout you, ma'am?" said Daly.

He looked pointedly at Amy Scarlett, who had by now staggered painfully to her feet.

"I ain't carryin' hardly any money," replied Amy. "Only what I'll need for my journey to 'Frisco."

"Oh, so yo're headin' for 'Frisco?"

"Yeah. I'm aimin' to catch a train at Laramie."

"Wa'al, I'll take that money, for you sure ain't gonna be needin' it."

"Whaddya mean?"

"You ain't goin' to 'Frisco. "Fact, you ain't goin' nowhere."

"Yo're plannin' to kill us, ain't you?" said Amy.

"'Course I am. Cain't afford to let any of you live," growled Daly.

"But we won't say nothin'. We ... we'll refuse to describe you. Honest! In fact, if you like, I'll swear as much on the Holy Bible!" wailed Harry Platt.

"Me, too," declared the banker.

Amy said nothing.

"Sorry, folks, cain't take that chance," said Daly. "Y'see, with you all dead, we're in the clear. As the newspapers say, nobody knows what we look like, or how many we number. We are completely untraceable. Which is why we haven't simply worn masks an' left it at that. Had we done so, then our victims could easily have told the law enough to put 'em on our trail."

"The Major is right," said Eli Judd. "They'd have given 'em our general descriptions, told 'em we were five in number, an' described our hosses. Then, it'd only have been a matter of time 'fore we was identified an' featured on 'Wanted' notices from Sheridan to Laramie."

"Pluggin' all our victims makes sure that don't happen," hissed Randy Wilkins, an evil glint in his eye.

"Yeah. This way, we remain what the papers have dubbed us, the Wyomin' Phantoms," said Daly.

"But surely . . ."

The banker got no further, for, as he spoke, Daly raised his gun and fired. The bullet struck the banker in the throat, severing his jugular vein and causing a fountain of crimson blood to spurt forth, most of it drenching his neighbour, the whiskey salesman. Then, a second shot, this time from Randy Wilkins, took out the banker's left eye and sent him crashing to the ground.

"Oh . . . oh, my God!" gasped Harry Platt.

He peered down at the bloodied corpse, watching the banker's life-blood slowly ebb away. It coloured the snow a bright shade of red, just as the last vestige of colour left the banker's and Platt's faces.

"Reckon it's yore turn," said Daly coldly. He glanced to his right. "You wanta finish him off, kid?" he asked.

"You bet!" cried the young gunslinger.

"No! Please! I . . . I'll g . . . give you any . . ."

Platt's words were abruptly ended

by the roar of Randy Wilkins' pearl-handled British Tranters. Two forty-five calibre slugs slammed into the whiskey salesman, knocking him off his feet and throwing him back a good couple of yards. He landed flat on his back in the snow, jerked once and then lay quite still.

"That leaves you, blondie," leered Daly. "Wa'al, I reckon we oughta have some sport 'fore we put out yore lights. Whaddya say, fellers?"

"Yeah. Ain't had me a woman in over a month," growled Bear, eyeing Amy lasciviously.

"Who gits first pickin's, that's what I wanta know?" said Elmer Judd.

"I do," retorted Daly flatly.

Nobody seemed disposed to argue.

"Wa'al, then, who's next?" enquired Eli Judd.

"You better draw lots between you," replied the bandit boss.

"Here! Wait a minute!" Amy Scarlett stared at the five desperadoes, a mixture of fear and loathing in her eyes. "So my morals ain't exactly above reproach. So I've sold my body in saloons an' bordellos from Wyomin' to Texas. But . . . but that don't make this right!" she declared angrily.

"You think we're bothered 'bout what's right?" sneered Daly, and he handed his Army Model Colt to Bear.

"You . . . you keep away from me!" screamed the blonde. "Sellin' myself or givin' myself freely is one thing. Bein' raped is quite another!"

"That's yore choice, blondie. You co-operate an' we can all have a good time. You try fightin' us an' yo're gonna git hurt," hissed Daly.

"Then, I'll git hurt!" cried Amy defiantly.

"I like that. A woman with spirit," he said.

Thereupon, he stepped forward and hit her. The sound of the slap resounded through the chill air and echoed across the plain. Daly held the blonde at arms-length so that she could not retaliate, and slapped her repeatedly until she sagged beneath the weight of his blows. As Amy teetered on the brink of unconsciousness, Daly ripped open the bodice of her dress. The shock of the icy wind biting into her naked breasts partially revived her, and Amy again began to struggle. But another vicious blow to the side of her face knocked out of her what little fight she had left. She slumped down onto the snow.

"I told you you should co-operate," said Daly.

The one-time Confederate officer dragged the semi-conscious woman through the snow towards the stagecoach. Then, he turned to Bear.

"Git them cadavers outta the coach," he growled.

"Sure thing, Major," replied Bear.

The giant outlaw climbed into the stagecoach and heaved the bodies of Jim Holt and the tall banker out, through the opposite doorway, onto the snow. In the meantime, Daly had succeeded in ripping off the remainder of Amy's clothing. And, so eager was he to ravish her voluptuous white body, that he completely forgot to empty the money from the blonde's reticule. It was left intact, lying among the heap of discarded clothes.

Joe Daly half-dragged, half-carried the naked woman up the steps and into the stagecoach. Then, he threw her down onto the floor and hastily unbuttoned his trousers. As he bared himself before her, Amy gasped, came too a little and recommenced struggling. But to no avail. A couple of vicious punches to the head dazed her, whereupon Daly brutally forced her legs apart and plunged down on top of her.

The blonde's moans and groans had no effect on her depraved, embittered attacker. Neither did they deter the others, who eagerly followed their leader's example. Lots were drawn and they threw themselves upon the woman one after another. The next to ravish Amy after Joe Daly was Eli Judd, then came Randy Wilkins, then Elmer Judd and finally the giant, Bear.

While Bear made the stagecoach rock with his exertions, Joe Daly was busy shooting the lock off the strongbox containing the wages intended for the J. B. Boxleiter Meat Processing Factory.

"Okay, fellers," he rasped. "Let's ram these banknotes into our saddlebags. We can have a proper share-out later."

"Yeah," agreed Eli Judd, rubbing his freezing-cold hands together. "We can do that some place nice 'n' warm."

"Where d'you reckon on aimin' for, Major?" asked Elmer Judd.

"Providence Flats," said Daly.

"Hows about headin' for 'Frisco?" suggested Randy Wilkins.

"Providence Flats is one helluva lot nearer," retorted the ex-Confederate officer, as he slipped a great wad of banknotes into one of his saddlebags. "It sure ain't as big as 'Frisco, but it's got all we want, plenty of women, whiskey an' gamblin'."

Wilkins shrugged his narrow shoulders and proceeded to open his second saddlebag.

"Okay. Whatever you say, Major," he said, with a grin. "Hell, are we gonna have ourselves some fun? You bet we are!"

As he and the other three shoved the last of the banknotes into their saddlebags, Bear finally emerged from the stagecoach. He stooped down and, picking up Harry Platt's discarded whiskey bottles, dropped them back into the carpet-bag.

"Guess you forgot these," growled the giant. "An' I figure we'll all need a few slugs 'fore we reach Providence Flats."

"Yeah. Bring 'em along, Bear," said Daly. He swung himself easily into the saddle, and then sat astride his chestnut gelding and calmly surveyed the scene of devastation he and his gang had wreaked. Then, staring across at Bear, he barked, "Finish off the woman, will you?"

Bear opened his mouth to say something. However, he changed his mind and, instead, muttered, "Er . . . yeah . . . sure thing, Major."

Joe Daly grinned and, wheeling round his horse, slowly set off across the snowbound prairie in the direction of Providence Flats. The others followed. Only Bear remained. He clambered back into the stagecoach.

Whereas the nineteen-year-old Randy Wilkins in his short, vicious life had already shot two women, Bear in his long, equally vicious life had killed none. It could not be said that he had much of a conscience, nor that he treated women well. He had no scruples about either beating or raping them. Yet there was something in the big man's make-up that made him reluctant to finish off the blonde. He could not have explained it, even to himself. He stared down at the naked woman, lying senseless on the floor of the stagecoach, and slowly drew the Remington from its holster.

The chill wind whistled through the doors and windows of the coach. Also, there was a hint of snow in the air. Bear grinned crookedly. He had had a sudden thought. There was no need to shoot the woman. She would freeze to death for sure. He aimed the revolver a couple of feet to the left of Amy's head and squeezed the trigger. The bullet thudded into the floorboards.

Clutching the carpet-bag full of whiskey bottles, Bear left the stagecoach. He glanced over his shoulder. Amy continued to lie motionless inside. Bear smiled to himself and climbed into the saddle. Then, he turned his roan's head and set off through the lightly falling snow in the wake of Major Joe Daly and the others.

3

JACK STONE peered through the swirling snow. It had begun to fall half an hour earlier. Now it was blowing a regular blizzard. Stone reckoned he had a good two hours' ride ahead of him before he would reach the staging-post at Bighorn Springs. He would rest up there till the storm blew itself out and then continue on his way south. He expected the stage was already there, and he smiled at the thought of enjoying a few warming drinks with his old army buddy, Bart Newton.

It was something of a shock, therefore, when suddenly, through the snowstorm, the Kentuckian came upon the abandoned stagecoach. Stone swiftly dismounted and, as he strode the few yards to the coach, he stumbled over something lying in a heap beneath a thin covering of snow. He crouched down and scrabbled away at the snow, and, to his horror, uncovered the body of the whiskey salesman, Harry Judd.

"Jeeze!" he hissed.

Jack Stone straightway realised what had happened. He felt cold inside. His guts churned. He knew that, if he looked hard enough, he would find other corpses hidden beneath the snow, and that one of them would be the body of his pal, Bart Newton. What had Bart called those murdering sonsofabitch? The Wyoming Phantoms. Well, wherever they had headed with their loot, there would be no tracking them. The falling snow had obliterated any trail they might have left.

The Kentuckian placed a hand on the open door of the stagecoach and heaved himself inside. The snow had blown in and a thin layer of it covered the seats and the floor. It also lay lightly upon the naked woman, who sprawled there unconscious. Stone knelt down beside her and, brushing away some of the snow, pressed his ear to her breast. He could just hear a faint beat of her heart. She was still alive!

Hastily, Stone retraced his steps the few yards to where his bay gelding stood. Thereupon, he promptly untied and removed his bed-roll. He also fished inside one of his saddlebags and pulled out a three-quarters full bottle of whiskey. He carried both the bed-roll and the whiskey bottle over to the stagecoach, and clambered back inside the coach.

Once more kneeling down beside the blonde, Stone roughly brushed off the remainder of the snow, then wrapped her in a blanket. He removed the cork from the whiskey bottle and, cradling Amy in his arms, forced open her mouth and poured a good slug of the amber liquor down her throat. The fiery liquid instantly revived her, causing her to cough and splutter. Slowly, she opened her eyes and gazed up into Stone's rugged features. Amy gasped. At once, she shrank back, a look of horror in her eyes.

"N . . . no!" she sobbed. "Not again! Please, not again!"

Stone had already guessed, from the fact that the woman was naked, that the outlaws who had held up the stagecoach had raped her.

"Don't worry, ma'am," he said quietly. "I ain't gonna hurt you."

"But you . . . you . . ."

"I ain't one of them dirty, no-account critters who shot up the stage an' forced theirselves on you, if that's what yo're thinkin'."

"Then . . . then, who . . . who are you?"

"Name's Stone. Jack Stone. I jest happened to be ridin' this way." The Kentuckian smiled gently at the blonde and asked, "You gotta name, ma'am?"

"Amy S . . . Scarlett."

"Wa'al, Miss Scarlett, I reckon the first thing is to git you outta here 'fore you catch yore death of cold."

"Y . . . yeah. I . . . I sure ain't

f . . . feelin' too good," replied Amy falteringly.

Stone nodded. He could see that. Amy's face was chalk-white and she was shivering violently beneath the blanket. Unless he could get her somewhere warm and dry pretty goddam quickly, she was likely to die from exposure. He forced some more whisky down Amy's throat. Then, lifting her up, still wrapped in the blanket, the Kentuckian carried her out into the snow.

"If 'n' you can hang on for a coupla hours more, there's a warm bed an' hot food an' drink awaitin' you at Bighorn Springs," he whispered into Amy's ear.

Amy had closed her eyes. But she remained conscious, and she nodded faintly.

"I . . . I'll try," she murmured.

"That's all I ask, ma'am," said Stone.

He laid the girl across the saddle of his horse and swiftly climbed up behind her. Then, cradling Amy in one arm and grasping the reins with his free hand, the Kentuckian set the gelding trotting off along the trail. Soon the stagecoach was blotted from sight by the driving snow. Stone gritted his teeth and urged the gelding into a gallop.

★ ★ ★

Stone had ridden faster than was either safe or wise in the conditions. But he was lucky and reached the staging-post at Bighorn Springs without mishap and well under the two hours he had expected to take.

The staging-post consisted of a log cabin, some stables and a corral. Stone dismounted in front of the cabin and lifted Amy down from the saddle. He rapped smartly on the cabin door and, without waiting for any response, pushed it open and stepped inside.

The room into which Stone stepped was in fact a bar-room. A long bar-counter faced him, and there was a small dining area situated at the far end of the room. A fire burnt merrily in the stone-built fireplace, close to the few tables and chairs which stood empty in the dining area. It seemed that, prior to Stone's arrival, the staging-post had had no customers that day. Stone was not surprised.

He carried Amy across the room and placed her in one of the chairs near the fire. The blanket slipped to reveal a smooth, velvety shoulder and one of the blonde's firm, milk-white breasts. Stone carefully pulled up the blanket to cover both and, at that moment, a small, bald-headed man entered the room from behind the bar-counter. He was elderly and ill-shaven, and he was wearing a rather grubby white apron.

"Howdy, stranger. You ain't seen the stage, have you? I expected it 'bout an hour back an' . . . " The Wells Fargo man paused, as he suddenly observed Amy slumped in the chair before the fire, Stone's snow-splattered blanket draped loosely round her naked body.

"What in tarnation . . . ?" he began.

"The stage has been held up an', as far as I can make out, this lady here is the sole survivor," said Stone.

"Holy cow!" The Wells Fargo man shook his head and asked, "Was it . . . was it them goddam Wyomin' Phantoms?"

"I reckon."

"Wa'al, then, I guess the lady was lucky."

"Lucky? Lucky to be raped an' . . . ?"

"No, 'course not. But lucky to be alive. This the fourth time they've held up a stage an' she's the first person outta all their victims who they ain't gunned down."

"Yeah, wa'al, she ain't gonna survive much longer if 'n' we don't git her blood circulatin'. She's near froze to death," said Stone.

"Okay. So, whaddya suggest?"

"You have a spare bed?"

"Sure."

"Lead me to it, an' then you go git both of us somethin' hot to eat."

"Hash an' beans, okay?"

"Some kinda soup'd be better for the lady."

"Okay."

Amy Scarlett had relapsed into unconsciousness during the ride through the snowstorm. Now it was Stone's urgent task to revive her. He carried her into the bedroom provided by the Wells Fargo man and removed the snow-sodden blanket. He sent the man to fetch some dry towels, then spent the next fifteen minutes drying Amy and rubbing life back into her. A couple of slugs of whiskey forced between her ice-cold lips completed the cure. Amy coughed, spluttered, shuddered convulsively and slowly opened her eyes.

"Where . . . where am I?" she mumbled.

"Safe an' sound in the Wells Fargo stagin'-post at Bighorn Springs," replied Stone, as he tucked her into bed.

Amy smiled faintly.

"I . . . I gotta lot to thank you for,

I guess," she murmured.

"Anyone would've done the same, Miss Scarlett," replied Stone.

"Yore name? Did you say it was Jack Stone?"

"Yup."

"I heard of you. Back in Sheridan. You got some reputation, Mr Stone."

"Which is why I ain't in the law business no more. These days I aim to stay outta trouble."

"Cain't say that I blame you."

"Yeah. Wa'al, don't you go tirin' yoreself talkin'. The feller that runs this here stagin'-post is cookin' you some soup. You take that an' then git yoreself some rest. A good night's sleep is what you need more than anythin'."

"Will you be here when I wake up?"

"Sure will."

"I . . . I'll look forward to renewin' our acquaintance."

Amy again smiled faintly and thereupon closed her eyes.

She woke when the soup arrived, but could manage only two or three mouthfuls. Then, she lay back in the bed and pushed the plate to one side.

When Stone was certain that Amy was sound asleep and breathing regularly, he headed back into the bar-room and settled down at one of the tables before the fire. A couple of minutes later, the Wells Fargo man appeared carrying two plates piled high with hash and beans. He then produced a coffee pot and two tin mugs.

"Guess you've earned this," he said to Stone.

Over supper the two men introduced themselves. The Wells Fargo man was Seth Lang, a one-time Indian scout like Stone. Therefore, as well as discussing the hold-up, they also reminisced a little about their experiences during the Indian wars. Then, when they had finished eating and were sitting in front of the fire quietly smoking cheroots, Seth Lang asked, "Okay, Mr Stone, so whaddya aim to do now? Stay the night an' then . . . ?"

Stone shook his head.

"Nope," he said. "I reckon it's my duty to report the hold-up to the sheriff in Casper. Also, I'd like to git a doctor out to look at Miss Scarlett as soon as possible."

"Hell, she ain't hurtin' none. A good night's sleep'll be all is needed to cure her," replied Lang.

"Mebbe. But remember she's been through some ordeal. My guess is them sons of a bitch were pretty darned rough with her. Anyways, I've made up my mind."

"Okay."

"I'll need a hoss. An' you can stable mine, an' feed an' curry it."

"Sure."

"I'll be back with the sheriff an' the doc as soon as I can make it. I'll settle with you then."

"Right."

Seth Lang walked across to the window and peered out into the gathering darkness. The snow was still falling thickly. Lang grimaced and turned to face the Kentuckian.

"I sure don't envy you yore ride," he said.

★ ★ ★

It was just after noon on the following day when Jack Stone returned to the staging-post at Bighorn Springs. The storm had long since abated and it was a bright, sunlit afternoon, though an icy wind still swept relentlessly across the wide open prairie.

Stone was accompanied by Casper's Sheriff Martin Bell, a large, red-faced man in his mid-forties; Doc Norris, elderly, thin as a rake and dressed funereally in black hat, coat and trousers; a dozen solemn-looking men recruited by the sheriff as his posse; and, last but certainly not least, US Marshal John Bannerman.

Bannerman was one of a number of US marshals based in Laramie, and he had been sent north with instructions to seek and find the outlaw gang, which, for the last couple of months, had been terrorising the territory, the gang dubbed by the newspapers the Wyoming Phantoms.

He was a man of about middle height, neither fat nor thin. Cool blue eyes peered out of a weatherbeaten, square-jawed face, the face of a man who had experienced all manner of challenges and dangers in his thirty-three years. A heavy sheepskin coat was worn over his brown, city-style, three-piece suit, a black string tie decorated the neck of his crisp white linen shirt, a brown Derby hat was placed on his head at a jaunty angle, and his smart brown leather boots gleamed in the bright sunshine. For weapons, Bannerman favoured a Colt Peacemaker on his right thigh and a Winchester in his saddleboot. All in all, he looked razor-sharp and brimming with confidence, a man who knew exactly where in life he was going.

Indeed, Bannerman was a most

ambitious fellow. The Chief Marshal at Laramie was due to retire in three months' time and Bannerman badly wanted his job. He knew that, should he succeed in tracking down the Wyoming Phantoms, he would do his chances of promotion a power of good. Therefore, he was determined to succeed at all costs.

He dismounted and, along with Stone, the sheriff and the doctor, stepped into Seth Lang's log cabin, where they were greeted with some relief by the Wells Fargo man. Lang explained straightaway that Amy had been gripped by a fever during the night and had become delirious.

"An' she ain't gittin' no better," he concluded gloomily. "You best see her, Doc."

Doc Norris nodded. He immediately disappeared with Lang into the bedroom, while the others waited silently in the bar-room. During their lengthy wait, Sheriff Martin Bell went outside and invited his posse to dismount and join them inside. It was not particularly warm in the bar-room, the fire being rather low. Nevertheless, it was a good deal warmer than outside in the snow, with the wind whistling across the seemingly endless prairie. Consequently, the dozen citizens of Casper, who had rallied to the sheriff's call, thankfully hustled into the bar-room.

"Wa'al?" said Sheriff Bell when Doc Norris reappeared.

The doctor shook his head. His expression, lugubrious at the best of times, was positively mournful.

"It ain't lookin' good," he said.

"Miss Scarlett is gonna be okay, ain't she?" said Stone.

"I dunno. It's touch 'n' go. Depends on whether her fever breaks in time. I've given her a draught of medicine, an' left sufficient with Seth here for her to have further draughts every four hours over the next few days. If the medicine works, the fever will break an' she'll likely be okay. If not . . . "

Doc Norris said no more, but simply shrugged his shoulders.

"An' there ain't nothin' more you can do?" asked Bannerman.

"Nope." Doc Norris smiled thinly and said, "I got other patients need tendin' back in Casper. So, I'd best be headin' back to town. I'll ride out again in a coupla days."

"One thing 'fore you go, Doc. Can I question her?" enquired Bannerman.

"Nope. You try that, you might easily kill her."

"I'll be gentle with her."

"Nope. She needs complete rest. You cain't disturb her, marshal."

"But she saw them goddam murderin' bastards. She's the only person ever to have survived one of their hold-ups. If 'n' she could describe 'em to me . . ."

"It ain't no good, marshal. I 'preciate you wanta catch them Wyomin' Phantoms. Hell, we all want them caught! But I really cain't permit you to put my patient's life at risk," said the doctor firmly.

"It's her life agin' the lives of God knows how many future victims of those cold-blooded killers," argued Bannerman.

"That's right!" cried one of the posse.

"It's worth the risk," added another.

"Sheriff you got the authority," said Bannerman.

"Wa'al, I dunno. I don't like to go agin' the doc," said Bell doubtfully.

"If 'n' you don't I reckon that, in my capacity as a US marshal, I'll jest have to take that responsibility," rasped Bannerman.

The sheriff hesitated. He was caught in two minds. However, before he could decide whether or not to overrule Doc Norris' embargo, Jack Stone intervened.

"That wouldn't be at all smart, marshal," said the Kentuckian.

"No?" snarled Bannerman.

"Nope. What kinda information d'you reckon you'll git from Miss Scarlett in her present condition? Probably all you'll git is the wild ravin's of a delirious woman. An' if, 'cause of yore questionin', her fever worsens an' she dies, then where will you be?"

"Wa'al . . ."

"You'll be without the one witness who could help you track down them murderin' varmints."

"So, whaddya reckon, Stone?"

"I reckon you should give the doc's medicine a chance to work."

"An' if it don't?"

"That's the chance you take. It's a gamble either way, but I figure that is yore best bet."

"Hmm."

Bannerman reflected on Stone's argument and finally, for he was no fool, he came to the same conclusion as the Kentuckian. Bannerman didn't like it, but that was how it was. He reluctantly nodded his head.

"You'll postpone yore questionin' till after Miss Scarlett recovers from her fever?" said a relieved Doc Norris.

"Guess so." Bannerman smiled grimly and shrugged his shoulders. Then he glanced across at the Kentuckian and growled, "Okay, wa'al, let's git on out to where you left that there stage, Stone."

"Sure."

The Kentuckian led the way out of the cabin. Then he, Bannerman, the sheriff and the sheriff's posse all remounted and set off along the trail in the direction of Buffalo. Doc Norris, meanwhile, headed back towards Casper, while Seth Lang remained at the staging-post, where he attended to his normal duties and, at the same time, kept a kindly eye on his fever-wracked guest.

4

IT took two whole days for the fever to break but when, eventually, Doc Norris returned to Bighorn Springs, he found Amy Scarlett sitting up in bed, wearing one of Seth Lang's nightshirts and tucking into a plate of pork and beans. He also found Jack Stone, US Marshal John Bannerman and, of course, the Wells Fargo man, all grouped round the blonde's bed.

As for Sheriff Martin Bell and his posse, they had long since returned to Casper. Bell had ordered that the bodies of the victims of the hold-up be placed inside the stagecoach and taken back to town for Christian burial. He had also gathered together their various portmanteaux and differing kinds of baggage, all of which had been broken open, ransacked and then abandoned by the outlaws. Most of it he had taken with him to Casper, but the two large trunks containing Amy Scarlett's clothing had been left at the staging-post, as had the reticule containing her travelling money. The sheriff had discovered this last item lying in the snow, hidden among the clothes which Joe Daly had ripped off Amy's body.

"Wa'al, Doc, whaddya think?" enquired Bannerman eagerly, as Norris entered the room.

Doc Norris ignored the marshal's question. He did, however, run a professional eye over the blonde.

"How do you feel, Miss Scarlett?" he asked quietly.

"Not too bad. A li'l weak, mebbe," replied Amy.

"Wa'al, when you've finished yore meal, I'll jest examine you to make sure that fever's well an' truly gone."

"An' then can I question her?" demanded Bannerman.

"Only if Miss Scarlett feels up to it," said Doc Norris.

"But, hell, them danged no-account

critters who held up the stage have already got over forty-eight hours' start on me!" exploded Bannerman.

"It's okay, marshal. I'll answer yore questions, for I know yo're mighty anxious to git onto their trail," said Amy.

"I sure am!" declared the marshal.

"Yes. Wa'al, Miss Scarlett, you jest finish yore meal first, an' take yore time. A few more minutes ain't gonna make no difference," said the doctor.

He waited until Amy had finished eating and then he turned the others out of the bedroom. Thereupon, he proceeded to give the blonde a thorough examination.

"Wa'al," he said, when presently he had completed it, "I guess yo're gonna be okay. The fever's all gone. Nevertheles, my advice is to take it easy for a few days."

"Okay, Doc. But, can you tell me when the next stage for Laramie is due to arrive in Casper?"

"The day affer tomorrow."

"Then, guess I'll rest up in Casper till it comes. Is there a decent hotel there?"

"Sure. Jamieson's Hotel ain't too bad. If you like, I'll take you back to town in my gig."

"Thanks, Doc. I'd 'preciate that." Amy sighed wearily and went on, "But, first, I guess I'd best oblige the marshal an' answer those questions he's so keen to ask me."

"As I said, only if you feel up to it," said Doc Norris.

"Cain't say that I do. Not really. But I reckon it's my duty. I owe it to my fellow-passengers an' everyone else them sonsofabitch have murdered."

"Okay, Miss Scarlett, then I'll leave you to dress. An' I'll inform Marshal Bannerman you'll be through directly."

Doc Norris smiled gently at the blonde and, gathering together his medical equipment, made his way out of the room. Left to her own devices, Amy chose a smart, dark green velvet gown from among the various items of clothing in her two trunks, and slowly began to dress.

When she appeared half an hour later in the bar-room, she looked more like her old self. Only the unnaturally pale face and the strained look in her blue eyes gave any indication of the ordeal she had so recently undergone.

She was greeted sympathetically by the four men, and straightaway Seth Lang offered her a whiskey, which she gladly accepted. She sipped the fiery amber liquid and, as the warm glow spread from the pit of her stomach up through her body, she took courage and turned to face John Bannerman.

"You wanted to ask me some questions," she said.

"That's right, Miss Scarlett," replied the marshal.

"So, whaddya wanta know?"

"I'd like you, first of all, to describe exactly what happened. From the moment the first shot was fired until eventually you were left naked and semi-conscious upon the floor of the stagecoach, where Mr Stone found you."

Amy nodded. In a low voice, almost a whisper, she proceeded to do as Bannerman had asked. She left out nothing in her description of the hold-up and its aftermath. As she described the murder of her various travelling-companions and ultimately her own barbaric treatment at the hands of the outlaws, her voice broke and tears streamed unchecked and unheeded down her cheeks.

When she had finished, there followed a stunned silence. The almost unbelievable savagery and ruthlessness of the so-called Wyoming Phantoms had shocked even such tough, experienced gun-fighters as Jack Stone and the marshal.

"Guess you've been through hell, Miss Scarlett," growled Stone.

"Yeah. An' I sure am sorry to have had to make you re-live that terrible ordeal," said Bannerman.

"That's okay, marshal," said Amy,

drying her eyes. "I'm gonna re-live it many more times, I guess, 'fore I can put it completely outta my mind. In fact, mebbe I never will."

"Oh, I'm sure you will, in time," said Doc Norris optimistically.

For a man who dressed so funereally and who normally wore such a lugubrious expression, the doctor was, surprisingly enough, the possessor of a naturally sunny and hopeful disposition.

"Wa'al, I hope so," said Amy.

"'Course you will," said Stone, and he smiled encouragingly at the blonde.

"But, for the present, I'm afraid I've still got some questions to put to you," said Bannerman.

Amy's face fell. But she summoned up her courage and, looking across at him, stared Bannerman straight in the eye.

"Ask away, marshal," she said quietly.

"Okay. Wa'al, you didn't say exactly how many outlaws there were. I kinda got the impression there were four or five of 'em," said the marshal.

"There were five altogether."

"An' can you describe 'em?"

"I ain't likely to forget the bastards who . . ."

"No, 'course not. So?"

"Their leader was a big feller, kinda handsome I s'pose, 'cept he had a livid white scar disfigurin' his left cheek. He wore the uniform of a soldier."

"A Union soldier?" asked Bannerman.

"Nope. A Confederate. An' the others addressed him as 'Major'. He seemed to have a natural authority 'bout him."

"I see. An' the others? Did any of them wear an unusual or distinctive form of dress?"

"Only one. He was no more 'n a boy. Mebbe eighteen or nineteen. A thin, vicious-lookin' young feller, he dressed all in black, an' his guns were kinda fancy."

"Fancy?"

"Yeah. They had pearl handles."

"He carried two handguns, then?"

"Yes."

"An' what about the rest?"

"There was two who looked like brothers. Short, stocky men, both of 'em heavily bearded." Amy shuddered at her recollection of their unspeakable treatment of her. "The fifth feller was a real giant. Enormous. An' he, too, was heavily bearded. I was 'bout to pass out at the time, so I cain't be certain, but I b'lieve the Major called him 'Bear'. He sure was built like a grizzly," she added.

"Okay. Them's pretty good descriptions. But is there anythin' else you can recollect hearin' that might help put me onto their trail?" asked Bannerman.

"Again I cain't be sure. I was pretty far gone."

"Never mind. Whaddya think you heard?"

"I think I heard the Major say they was gonna head for Providence Flats."

John Bannerman whistled. He knew the reputation of that notorious hell-hole. A town beyond the law. If the

Wyoming Phantoms were holed up there, they would take some dislodging. A whole posse of US marshals would be needed to bring them out of Providence Flats. And even that might not be enough.

"If 'n' they're hidin' out there, yo're gonna have some job flushin' them out," commented Stone, echoing the marshal's thoughts.

"I already figured that one," retorted Bannerman.

"So, whaddya plan doin', marshal?" enquired Seth Lang.

"I plan to saddle up an' head on out there."

"To Providence Flats? On yore own?" Lang shook his head disbelievingly.

"You surely ain't aimin' to go agin' them varmints on yore own? Hell, the odds are five to one you won't make it," added Doc Norris.

Bannerman smiled quietly.

"I ain't proposin' to take 'em on," he said. "Jest to establish that they're actually there."

"An' then what?" asked Amy.

"I dunno for sure. I gotta think that one out. An' I shall have plenty of time for thinkin' while I'm ridin' out there. Providence Flats must be at least fifty miles from here. Ain't that right, Lang?"

The Wells Fargo man nodded. He sipped his whiskey and declared, "Nearer sixty, I should say."

Bannerman turned to the Kentuckian.

"You wanta come along, Stone?" he asked. "I could do with a man of yore calibre, to back me up in case of trouble."

Stone shook his head.

"Nope," he said. "I try to steer clear of trouble these days."

"Jest thought you might want to revenge yore friend's death. You did say the shotgun guard was an old army pal of yourn, didn't you?" said Bannerman.

"I did, an' I intend to pay my last respects when I reach Casper. But I ain't gittin' involved. I'll leave the catchin' of his killers to you an' yore feller law-officers."

"Fair enough." Bannerman rose from his stool in front of the bar-counter and shrugged on his sheepskin coat. He threw back the remains of his whiskey and, taking one last puff at his cheroot, dropped it onto the floor and ground it out beneath the heel of his boot. "Wa'al, folks," he said, "I'll say adios. Jest one thing more before I go, though. Where are you aimin' for, Miss Scarlett?"

"My plan was to take the stage as far as Laramie, an' then catch the train to 'Frisco." Amy smiled wanly. "That still is my plan. I'm gonna start up a business in 'Frisco, y'see." Again she smiled. "A respectable business," she added wryly.

Bannerman returned the blonde's smile.

"Wa'al, I wish you luck," he said. "But do me a favour, an', when you reach Laramie, make sure you pay a call on Chief Marshal Blake in the

US marshals' office. Tell him that I'm headin' on out to Providence Flats an' will be in touch. An' give him yore address in 'Frisco. I s'pose you do know where 'bout you'll be stayin' in 'Frisco?"

"Yes."

"Wa'al, give him the address, for we may need you as prosecution witness at the trial of that murderin' sonofabitch of a Confederate major an' his gang."

"You aimin' to bring 'em in alive, then, marshal?" asked the blonde.

"If I can. I wanta see those bastards swing," said Bannerman.

"They sure deserve to," added Doc Norris fervently.

"Yeah," said Stone. "I'll go along with that. But you take care, marshal. They seem to be a mighty dangerous bunch."

"I will." Bannerman smiled grimly. He clapped his brown Derby at its usual rakish angle on his head and stepped outside. Then he paused, turned and, before closing the door behind him,

glanced back and addressed the blonde.
"Be seein' you at their trial, Miss Scarlett," he said confidently.

Thereupon, he slammed the door shut and was gone.

Stone drew hard on his cheroot and exhaled a thin stream of smoke.

"I hope the marshal realises jest what he's takin' on," he drawled, "for it sure as hell ain't gonna be easy catchin' them murderin' varmints."

"Oh, Bannerman is a pretty shrewd feller, Mr Stone," said Doc Norris. "I guess he knows what he's doin'."

"Yeah? Wa'al, I don't reckon I'll be around to find out how he makes out," said the Kentuckian.

"Where are you headin' for, then?" enquired Amy.

"I'm ridin' south to Texas."

"I see. Reckon you'll be goin' by way of Casper an' Laramie?"

"S'right, ma'am."

"In that case, could I beg a favour?"

"Name it."

"The doc here has offered to give me

a ride into Casper, where I aim to wait for the next stage. But I gotta admit I'm kinda nervous 'bout travellin' by stage."

"That's only to be expected after yore recent experience," said Doc Norris.

"Yes. So, I was wonderin' whether you'd be prepared to wait in Casper with me, Mr Stone, an' then accompany me as far as Laramie?" said Amy. "I'd feel a whole heap happier havin' a man with yore reputation along to protect me."

"It'll be my pleasure, Miss Scarlett," said Stone.

"I . . . I'd be prepared to pay for inconveniencin' you," said Amy.

"There ain't no call for that. I'm in no desperate hurry to reach Texas. Hell, I got all winter to git there."

"Even so, yo're gonna have to put up some place till the stage comes in. So, you must at least let me pay yore expenses as far as Laramie."

Stone considered this. He had only a few dollars in his pocket, whereas it was evident the blonde was pretty well-heeled. He would be a fool to refuse her offer.

"Okay," he said. "I'd 'preciate that."

"We'll both stop-over at Jamieson's Hotel in Casper. The doc recommends it. Ain't that right, Doc?"

"It is, Miss Scarlett." Doc Norris rose and picked up his hat. "Wa'al, I guess we oughta be gittin' along now, if we're to reach Casper 'fore nightfall," he said.

Ten minutes later, he and Amy were installed in his gig, Amy's two trunks were stashed aboard and his grey mare was trotting off in the direction of Casper. Jack Stone's bay gelding loped along beside the gig, the big Kentuckian swaying easily in the saddle, the collar of his sheepskin coat turned up against the chill Wyoming wind that continued to sweep across the bleak, snowladen landscape.

5

JOHN BANNERMAN reached Providence Flats on the evening of the following day. He was cold, tired and hungry. But now he knew what he had to do. If he found the Wyoming Phantoms in town, he had to lure them out of it.

His plan, thought out on the ride from Bighorn Springs, was a simple one. He would pose as an embittered bank employee, a man who had been passed over for promotion. He would let it be known that he knew when the next consignment of money was to be transferred by wagon from the West and Frontier Bank at Laramie to Fort Henderson, where it was to pay the garrison wages. And he would also let it be known that he was looking for a gang of men to help him hold up the wagon. He intended to approach one of the outlaws described by Amy Scarlett with this information. He did not doubt that the gang would rise to the bait. Then it would be an easy matter, he reckoned, to lead the bastards into the trap he had planned for them.

Bannerman checked in at the only hotel in town, a run-down, two-storey frame building, with the paint peeling from the outside walls and several layers of dirt and dust decorating its gloomy interior. It was most inappropriately named the Grand Hotel. He left his horse at the livery stables attached to the hotel, with instructions that the animal should be curried, watered, fed and rested, and then made his way along the sidewalk to the nearest of Providence Flats' four saloons.

The Golden Garter was the largest saloon in town and the most popular. It was owned by a one-time bank robber called Frank Cassidy, who was finding fleecing his fellow desperadoes far easier and more profitable than bank robbery had ever been. Roulette, blackjack and poker were the three games of chance on offer, and all seemed mighty popular. The tables were all fully occupied and the crowd surrounding the roulette wheel was four deep.

Bannerman pushed through the batwing doors and stepped inside the huge bar-room-cum-gaming-hall. Tobacco-smoke swirled round in the light cast by the numerous kerosene lamps hanging from the rafters, on a small stage a girl in a red dress sang to the accompaniment of a honky-tonk piano, the solid mahogany bar-counter was awash with spilt beer and whiskey, and the four bartenders behind it were being kept mighty busy with the constant demands of the large crowd of drinkers.

Bannerman glanced up at the railed walkway which ran round the upper level of the saloon. Various customers climbed up the stairway leading to this, arm-in-arm with Frank Cassidy's 'young ladies', and then disappeared into the bedrooms that opened off it. As Bannerman watched, he spied a youth, thin and weedy-looking, and dressed all in black, vanish with a small, plump brunette into one of the bedrooms. Bannerman grinned. The youth fitted exactly the description given to him by Amy Scarlett, even down to the two pearl-handled revolvers in his holsters. He might not be one and the same person, but Bannerman figured that he probably was.

The marshal sauntered across to the bar and positioned himself at one end, close to a huge, pot-bellied stove. There were four such stoves placed at strategic points around the saloon. The heat generated by these and by the great press of people in the saloon contrasted markedly with the sub-zero temperature outside.

"What's yore pleasure, sir?" demanded a voice from behind Bannerman's left shoulder.

Bannerman turned and found himself facing a slim, swarthy-looking man, neatly attired in a black city-style suit, sparkling white shirt with a ruffled collar, neat black tie, dark green brocade vest and highly-polished black leather shoes. The man had about him an air of quiet authority and, while his brown eyes twinkled with good humour, nonetheless Bannerman guessed he would be a bad man to cross. He regarded the marshal with a quizzical eye.

"What's yore pleasure, sir?" he repeated.

"I'm jest passin' through is all," replied Bannerman. "Figured on havin' me a few drinks 'fore I turned in for the night."

"Wa'al, we got more to offer than jest drink."

"Yeah, I had noticed, Mr ... er ... Mr ... ?"

"Cassidy. Frank Cassidy. I own this here establishment."

"Congratulations, Mr Cassidy. You got yoreself a reg'lar gold-mine, I reckon."

"It earns me a dollar or two. An' what's yore line of business, sir? I ... er ... don't think you said yore name?"

"John Bannon." Bannerman pulled a rueful face and said, "I'm afraid I'm jest a simple, ordinary clerk workin' in Laramie. I've been to see my sick mother in Buffalo an' am now on my way back to Laramie."

"I see. Wa'al, I hope yore mother is gittin' better, Mr Bannon."

"She is, I'm glad to say."

"Then, why don't you celebrate a li'l? If 'n' you fancy a nice, accomdatin' young woman ..."

"No. No, I don't think so. I'll jest settle for a few quiet drinks."

"Okay, Mr Bannon. As you wish."

Cassidy smiled and strolled off towards one of the poker tables, where he paused to watch the play. He pulled a cigar from the top pocket of his jacket and proceeded to light it. Then he glanced back towards the bar-counter, where he watched Bannerman ordering a whiskey.

"A simple, ordinary clerk, my ass!" he muttered.

Bannerman, meantime, was enjoying the sensation of the fiery liquor hitting his stomach and sending a warm glow coursing through his veins. He had got darned cold on his long ride to Providence Flats.

His plan had been to tour the saloons and bordellos until he came upon the men described by Amy Scarlett and then engage them in conversation. He had realised that he would be lucky to find all five of them together, and had determined to approach however many of them he did find. Now he was not sure what to do. Should he follow through his original plan, or should he remain where he was and accost the youth in black when he returned downstairs? He pondered this question for a few minutes. Then, finally, he determined to give the youth an hour to re-emerge. If, within that span of time, he did not come downstairs,

Bannerman would quit the Golden Garter and commence his search for the other members of the gang.

The next fifty minutes were spent pleasantly enough. During the course of this period, Bannerman consumed four whiskies and listened appreciatively to the girl singer. She had a melodious voice and was, in addition, a very pretty young woman and a delight to watch. Bannerman also kept an eye open for the saloon-keeper, but Cassidy made no attempt to resume their conversation. He seemed to be wholly occupied in roaming slowly round the bar-room and checking that all was well at the various tables.

Bannerman removed the gold hunter from his vest pocket. He studied it carefully. Ten more minutes and he would have to leave the warmth of the Golden Garter and brave the bitter cold of draughty Main Street on his way to the next saloon. But it was not to be, for, as Bannerman returned the watch to his vest pocket, so a bedroom door opened upstairs and the youth in black stepped out onto the railed walkway.

The marshal watched him descend the stairway and head across to the bar-counter. Bannerman waited. The youth stood only a few feet away and ordered a beer. Bannerman continued to wait. Then, just as the youth raised the glass to his lips, he left his position at the end of the bar and deliberately jostled the youth with his elbow.

"What the hell?" exclaimed the youth, as a quantity of his beer spilled onto the floor.

"I do apologise!" cried Bannerman.

"You clumsy lunkhead! I oughta fill you full of lead!"

"I . . . I said I'm sorry. An' I'm willin' to git you another beer. Another two or three if you like."

The youth eyed Bannerman angrily. But the contrite look in the marshal's eye and his generous offer seemed to placate the youth.

"Okay. Fill it up," he said, gulping down the remains of the beer and handing Bannerman the empty glass.

"Certainly."

"You should be more careful. Folks in this town take offence pretty darned quick."

"I guess they do at that."

"You know the kinda folks who inhabit Providence Flats?" enquired the youth.

"Yeah, I know. That's why I'm here."

"Whaddya mean?"

"I . . . I'm lookin' for help, the kinda help a man'd expect to find in a place like Providence Flats."

"Really? An' what kinda help would that be?"

"I dunno that I oughta say." Bannerman passed the youth a full glass of foaming beer. "It . . . it's not for jest anyone's ears," he added earnestly.

"If 'n' you don't say, how d'you expect to git any help?" demanded the youth.

"You gotta point. I . . . I guess I

have to tell someone."

"So, why not me?"

"Wa'al, Mr . . . er . . . ?"

"Randy Wilkins. You heard of me?"

"No, cain't say I have."

Wilkins' face dropped. Before joining Joe Daly and his gang, he had been wanted for murder in no fewer than three states, and he was proud of his notoriety. Therefore, he was quite disappointed that Bannerman had not heard of him.

"I'm a much-wanted man," he boasted.

"I daresay you are. But, then, I ain't much-travelled. I don't often hear of any news outside of what's happenin' in Laramie. So, what kinda line are you in, Mr Wilkins?"

"At present, I'm makin' myself a li'l money holdin' up stages."

"On yore own?"

"Nope. That's too darned risky."

"So, you have some friends who ride along with you?"

"'S'right." Wilkins narrowed his eyes

and glared at the marshal. "Hell, I'm the one who's s'posed to be askin' the questions!" he hissed.

"I . . . I didn't mean to pry, but, y'see, as luck would have it, I'm lookin' for a gang who specialise in holdin' up stages," said Bannerman. He placed a hand on Wilkins' shoulder and drew him apart from the crowd round the bar. Then he whispered quietly into the youth's ear, "I gotta plan to make me mighty rich. Me an' whoever helps me."

"How many men d'you need?" asked Wilkins.

"Four or five, I guess."

"I take it you ain't broached nobody else with this here plan of yourn?"

"Nope. Only other feller I've spoken to is the saloon-keeper."

"Frank Cassidy?"

"That's him. I spun him a tale 'bout havin' been visitin' my sick mother in Buffalo. Told him I was jest a simple, ordinary clerk back in Laramie."

"An' ain't you?"

"Nope. I'm assistant manager at Laramie's branch of the West an' Frontier Bank."

Randy Wilkins whistled softly.

"That a fact?" he murmured.

"Yup. An' I got some information 'bout a consignment of money destined for Fort Henderson. Enough to pay the wages of the entire garrison for the last three months."

"Jeeze, that oughta add up to several thousand dollars!"

"It does. Wa'al, are you interested?"

"I could be. But first I gotta consult with my pardners."

"'Course. They're all here in Providence Flats, I s'pose?"

"You s'pose right."

"So, how 'bout introducin' me to 'em? John Bannon's the name, by the way."

Bannerman extended his hand and the pair shook hands. Then Randy Wilkins drained his second glass of beer. His thin, pale face contorted into a scowl, as he carefully considered the other's request. Finally, he shook his head.

"Nope," he said. "You wait here, Mr Bannon. I'll speak with 'em an' then, if they're interested, I'll come an' fetch you."

"An' if they ain't interested?"

"I'll come anyways, an' tell you. But I reckon they will be interested. Meantime, don't you go invitin' nobody else to join in yore li'l game. I sure wouldn't like that." And Wilkins smiled coldly and dropped his hands onto the pearl butts of his British Tranters.

"No, I won't do that," promised Bannerman.

He watched the black-clad gunslinger thread his way through the crowd and then push open the batwing doors and vanish into the night. Bannerman smiled quietly to himself. He had baited his hook and it seemed that the fish were about to bite. He turned and, leaning against the mahogany bar-counter, promptly ordered himself a celebratory drink.

★ ★ ★

Randy Wilkins found his boss in the Lucky Chance Saloon, fifty yards away on the opposite side of Main Street. There was no music and no roulette. A much smaller, quieter saloon than Frank Cassidy's establishment, it was favoured mostly by professional poker-players. A few quiet words in Joe Daly's ear were sufficient to persuade the ex-Confederate officer to throw in his hand and leave the game in which he was engaged. His fellow players muttered their protests, for he was ahead at the time. But none made too much of a fuss. Joe Daly was not a man any of them wanted to rile.

Daly steered the youth to the bar which, in contrast to that at the Golden Garter, was practically deserted. He ordered a whiskey for himself and a beer for Wilkins. Then, when the bartender had served him and wandered off to the far end of the bar-counter, he murmured, "This feller you spoke of, d'you reckon he's on the level?"

"I dunno," confessed Wilkins. "But what have we got to lose jest listenin' to him? If 'n' he is on the level, this could be our biggest haul yet."

"That's true," said Daly.

"D'you wanta speak to him on yore own, Major, or shall I find the others an' . . . ?"

"Yeah; find the others. I b'lieve Eli an' Elmer are playin' the wheel in the King of Diamonds, while Bear's most likely havin' hisself a good time with a coupla Ma Rainey's gals."

"Okay. I'll fetch 'em. But what about Bannon? Shall I send him along?"

"Nope. You jest find the others."

"Right, Major."

Joe Daly rubbed at the thin, livid scar that ran down his left cheek. His handsome face was as though carved from marble, his eyes ice-cold, matching the weather outside. So, this Bannon gent had come to Providence Flats looking to find some fellers to stage a hold-up. He had certainly come to the right spot. But, how had he set about recruiting his gang? He hadn't, strictly speaking. He had simply had a chance encounter with Randy Wilkins and, in the course of their subsequent conversation together, had blurted out his story. He had been looking for a gang of four or five desperadoes, and it happened that Randy belonged to such a gang. He had been looking specifically for hold-up specialists, not bank robbers or train robbers. And again it happened that Randy's gang specialised in robbing stagecoaches. One whole heap of coincidences! But Joe Daly did not much believe in coincidence.

The one-time Confederate glanced along the bar-counter. Perched on a stool and slumped across the marbled bar-top, his head resting in his arms, was the town drunk, an erstwhile gunslinger and cattle rustler who had long since lost his nerve. Mickey Pullen was slowly, inexorably drinking himself to death. Daly strolled along the bar and tapped the drunk on the shoulder.

"Howdy, Mickey, how's it goin'?" he asked cheerfully.

Mickey Pullen half-raised his head and viewed Daly with a curious red-rimmed eye. His vision was blurred and it was a moment or two before he could focus properly. Upon realising who had addressed him, he straightaway heaved himself into an upright position. Swaying precariously on the stool, he stammered, "Oh . . . it . . . it's goin' okay, M . . . Major."

"Glad to hear it, Mickey."

Pullen was as nervous as he was curious. Providence Flats was filled to overflowing with the dregs of society. Murderers rubbed shoulders with bandits. Confidence tricksters played poker with cattle rustlers. Petty thieves drank whiskey with mountebanks and gambling men. Professional killers exchanged banter with professional whores. But, of all those crowded into that hell-town, none had a more fearsome reputation for cold-blooded ruthlessness than that tall, handsome Southern gentleman, Major Joe Daly. Hence Mickey Pullen's nervousness.

"Is . . . is there anythin' I can do for you, Major?" he asked anxiously.

Daly beamed at the drunk.

"There is, Mickey. A small favour."

"'Course, Major. Whatever it is."

"I jest want you to step over to the Golden Garter an' ask Mr Cassidy if he'll oblige me with a few minutes of his time. Will you do that for me, Mickey?"

"Straight away, Major."

Daly grinned, as he watched the drunk weave an erratic path to the door. 'Straight away,' Mickey had said. That was a joke. Mickey's route to the Golden Garter was likely to be about as straight as the proverbial corkscrew.

"A bottle of whiskey," he rasped. "For Mickey when he gits back."

Before Mickey Pullen could return, the Judd brothers pushed their way in through the batwing doors and joined their leader. He ordered another bottle of whiskey and five glasses. Then, he and the brothers carried these across to an empty table in one corner of the bar-room. It was there that they were joined a few minutes later by Randy Wilkins and Bear. The youth fetched himself a beer (he rarely drank whiskey) and sat down with the others. The whiskey glasses were filled and those who smoked, the Major, the Judd brothers and Bear, all lit cheroots. It was thus that Frank Cassidy found them, quietly smoking and drinking.

"Sit down, Frank," said Daly genially and, pointing at the whiskey bottle, he added, "help yoreself to a drink."

"Th . . . thanks, Major." Cassidy, no less nervous than Mickey Pullen had been, poured his drink with a not entirely steady hand.

"There's a bottle on the bar for you, Mickey," said Daly.

The drunk's red-rimmed eyes glinted with pleasurable anticipation and his reddened, bloated features split into a wide smile.

"Gee, thanks, Major!" he gasped, and he happily made his unsteady way to the bar.

"You . . . er . . . wanted to see me," said Cassidy.

"Yes." Daly blew a circle of smoke into the air. "I have a very high opinion of you, Frank."

"Indeed?"

"Oh, yes! Yo're a man who keeps his finger on the pulse. A man who knows what's goin' on."

"I . . . I'm not sure I'm altogether with you, Major."

"The Golden Garter. That's yore territory, Frank."

"Wa'al, I own it."

"An' there ain't nothin' goin' on there that you don't know about."

"I keep a sharp eye on my croupiers an' the girls. I gotta, otherwise they'd cheat me for sure."

"An' yore customers. Do you keep a sharp eye on them?"

Frank Cassidy nodded. He glanced across the table at Randy Wilkins. He was beginning to get the drift of Joe Daly's conversation.

"Is it 'bout one partickler customer you wanta ask me?" he enquired, with a sly grin.

"You got it."

"The feller who spilt Randy's drink an' then engaged him in conversation?"

"Right."

"Whaddya wanta know, Major?"

"He said that he'd spoken to you earlier," intervened Wilkins.

"He did," agreed Cassidy.

"Told you some tale 'bout him bein' a clerk an' visitin' his sick mother in Buffalo. Said his name was John Bannon."

"That's right, Randy."

"Wa'al, that's interestin'." Daly smiled grimly. "Randy hadn't mentioned that you'd spoken to him. I jest guessed that you'd've kept a close eye on him, him bein' a stranger in town. But, if 'n' you've spoken to him, wa'al, I figure you probably got some idea of what he's up to. A shrewd feller like you, you must have. So, whaddya say, Frank?"

"He sure ain't no clerk, Major."

"No?"

"Nope."

"An assistant bank manager, mebbe?"

"Nope."

"Yo're a pretty good judge of character, Frank. Hell, you've got a reputation for it! So, whaddya reckon he is, then?"

Joe Daly leant forward and looked hard into the saloon-keeper's eyes. Cassidy did not flinch, but calmly returned the outlaw's gaze.

"I reckon he's a lawman," said Cassidy quietly.

"Why d'you reckon that?" demanded Daly.

"I got a feelin', an intuition. I cain't explain it, but I ain't often wrong, Major."

"No, I don't imagine you are."

"I can smell the law. I swear I can. An' Bannon had that kinda smell."

"Hmm." Daly leant back in his chair and took a long, satisfying puff at his cheroot. "Okay, Frank, thanks for yore time," he drawled.

Cassidy rose, relieved to find that his ordeal was over. In the event, it had been nothing much to get worried about. But, then, he always felt uneasy in the Major's company. The man exuded a positive aura of menace.

"D'you want me to keep an eye on him?" he asked. "I can put one of my men onto . . ."

Daly shook his head.

"No," he said. "That won't be necessary." He turned to Randy Wilkins. "Randy, you accompany Frank back to the Golden Garter, will you? An' then fetch Mr Bannon. I wanta hear what he's gotta say for hisself."

"Okay, Major."

Daly watched the pair cross the sawdusted floor of the Lucky Chance and push through the batwing doors. Then, he turned to face the others.

"I don't like it," he growled.

"What don't you like, Major?" asked Eli Judd.

Daly repeated what Randy Wilkins had told him and concluded, "If this feller is on the level, we cain't afford to turn him down. But I don't b'lieve he is. An' Frank . . ."

"Was guessin'. He don't know nothin'," said Bear.

"Nope, he don't. However, I trust Frank Cassidy's instincts."

"Mebbe. But nobody guesses right every time," commented Elmer Judd.

"Bannon's bumpin' into Randy like that, it was jest too neat," replied Daly, and he went on to explain the string of coincidences which made him doubtful as to whether their meeting had been entirely accidental.

"If, as you seem to suspect, Bannon engineered that meetin', then whaddya reckon, Major?" asked Eli Judd.

"He could be a lawman on Randy's trail. Randy's wanted for murder in more 'n one state," growled Bear.

"But why involve us?" said Daly.

Unless it's us he's after," suggested Eli Judd.

"How could he be?" demanded his brother. "Nobody knows what in hell we look like."

"That's right," said Bear.

Joe Daly scowled. Kill all witnesses. That had been his golden rule. And they had . . . hadn't they? Of course they had.

"No," he said quietly. "Nobody knows."

But he wondered.

A little more rather aimless conversation followed, but they got no further in their deliberations. Then Randy Wilkins reappeared, accompanied by John Bannerman. Daly waved Bannerman into a seat, but did not offer him a drink. Instead, he subjected the marshal to a long, penetrating stare.

"I b'lieve you have a proposition to put to us," he said finally.

"Has Randy already told you 'bout the pay-roll destined for the garrison at Fort Henderson?" enquired Bannerman.

"He has."

"Wa'al, I know how an' when it's

to be transported from our bank in Laramie to the fort."

"Do you indeed?"

"Yes. So, if yo're interested . . . ?"

"Oh, I'm interested!" Daly smiled coldly. "Yo're darned tootin' I'm interested!"

"In that case, ain't you gonna introduce yoreself?"

"Not at this stage. You know Randy's name. As for the rest of us, we'll jest stay anonymous till we've heard you out."

"If that's the way you wanta play it."

"It is, Mr Bannon. Therefore, if you'll kindly explain what you have in mind, I'd be obliged to you."

"Very well." Bannerman shrugged his shoulders and began, "My plan is a simple one, but, for it to work, I need four or five men who have experience of stagin' hold-ups, men who ain't afraid to shoot to kill."

"That 'bout sums us up," grinned Wilkins.

"In that case, listen an' listen carefully. On either Wednesday or Thursday next a closed wagon loaded with the Fort Henderson pay-roll will leave the bank at Laramie bound for the fort. It will have one driver an' an escort of one lieutenant an' half a dozen troopers. Now . . ."

"I thought you said you knew when this wagon was to leave Laramie?" said Daly.

"I do."

"Wednesday or Thursday next. Jeeze, that ain't very precise!" exclaimed Elmer Judd.

"'Cause the precise details ain't decided yet. My plan is that you fellers should ride out to Lone Pine Gulch an' hole up at that abandoned trapper's cabin there. You know the spot?"

Daly nodded.

"Okay, then. You hole up there while I ride into Laramie an' check what's goin' on. I'll git the exact timin's an' ride back out on Tuesday night."

"You sure you can git the exact timin's?" enquired Bear.

"'Course. In my capacity as assistant bank manager, I'm privy to that kinda information."

"Then what?" said Bear.

"Why, you fellers lie in wait for the wagon. Lone Pine Gulch should be jest perfect for an ambush. You plan it right an' I don't s'pose them soldiers will have a chance."

"Guess not," said Daly. "But what are you expectin' to git outta all this?"

"One sixth share of yore haul," said Bannerman.

"How? We ain't gonna hang around, y'know."

"You can bury my share beneath the floorboards in the trapper's cabin. I'll pick it up later."

"Yo're mighty trustin', ain't you?"

"I don't think you'll double-cross me."

"No?"

"Nope. After all, this could be but the

first of a number of such arrangements. Havin' a man, in my position an' with my knowledge as yore informant, would surely be a boon to a man in yore line of business?"

"That's true."

"We'd need to be careful, of course."

"So that no suspicion falls on you?"

"Exactly."

"Wa'al, Mr Bannon, I gotta confess yore plan seems foolproof. There's jest one thing, though. Why are you doin' this? I shouldn't've thought a man in yore position would have needed to . . ."

Bannerman interrupted the Major with an angry wave of his arms. Anger clouded his eyes as he spoke. He was nothing if not a good actor.

"I'm doin' it 'cause I've been treated shabbily, goddam shabbily, by the bank," he rasped.

"Oh, yeah?"

"Yeah. Let me explain. The previous manager of the Laramie branch was also a director of the bank. Wa'al, three years back, he brought in his son to learn the business. A smart enough young feller, I must say. Quick to learn an' mighty ambitious. However, he ain't got nothin' like my experience an' years of service."

"No, I guess not."

"So, when his father got a transfer to bank headquarters in 'Frisco, I naturally enough expected to succeed to his job as manager of the Laramie branch."

"But you didn't?"

"Nope. The post went to the son. I remain assistant manager," Bannerman scowled. "Does that strike you as fair?" he asked.

"Cain't say it does," replied Daly.

"Which is why I'm gonna git my own back. Four or five hold-ups carefully planned an' executed over the next coupla years an' I'll have enough money to retire from bankin'."

"You supply the information an' we do the jobs, is that it?"

"Right."

"An' you think you can escape suspicion?"

"I think so. Anyways, that's the risk I'm prepared to take."

Joe Daly glanced round the faces at the table. All of them looked expectantly at him. It was evident they believed Bannon's tale and were keen to make a play for the Fort Henderson pay-roll. They were simply waiting for his say-so.

"Wa'al, boys," he said, "whaddya think? Do we oblige Mr Bannon?"

"Sure," growled Bear eagerly. "We'd be crazy not to."

Daly glanced at Randy Wilkins.

"That yore opinion, too, kid?" he asked.

"Yup," replied the youth.

"An' mine," added Elmer Judd.

"An' mine," agreed his brother.

Daly nodded. But he was still not convinced. Bannon seemed to be on the level. His story was certainly plausible. Yet Daly could not forget Frank Cassidy's words. And he recalled that, twice before in the last few months, Cassidy had picked out lawmen who had ridden into the town incognito on the trail of wanted men.

"I dunno," he said.

"Aw, come on, Major!" cried Bear. "You cain't seriously propose we pass up a chance like this!"

Daly glared at the bearded giant. He did not like anyone to dispute his authority. He was boss and what he said was final.

"You thinkin' on takin' over as boss, are you, Bear?" he hissed. "You gonna make the decisions from now on?"

"No," replied Bear. 'Course not. But, hell, the Fort Henderson pay-roll! That's one helluva lotta dollars!"

"Yeah, guess it is at that," sighed Daly.

He was sorely tempted Perhaps Cassidy's instincts had let him down for once. Anyway, there was one way to be sure. If Bannon was a lawman, he would be carrying a badge somewhere on his person, or maybe among his belongings. Daly grinned savagely.

"Frank Cassidy seems to think yo're a lawman," he said. "Wa'al, assumin' you ain't, I don't s'pose you'd mind us searchin' to see whether yo're carryin' a badge?"

"'Course not," said Bannerman. "I 'preciate you cain't be too careful."

The marshal smiled happily in the knowledge that his badge was safely hidden in a small compartment cut into the bottom of the stock of his Winchester. He reckoned, therefore, that the chances of the outlaws discovering it were pretty remote.

As Bannerman spoke, the batwing doors of the saloon flew open and a muffled figure burst in. The man had clearly only just ridden into town, for he was wearing a bearskin coat over his buckskins and had a poncho draped across his shoulders. He stamped his feet up and down and beat his arms together in an attempt to warm himself. Then, he pulled his Stetson up from over his ears and headed towards the bar-counter.

"Goddam it!" cried the stranger, stopping abruptly in the centre of the bar-room and staring wild-eyed at the corner-table where Joe Daly and his gang sat. "I cain't believe it!" he declared. "US Marshal John Bannerman as I live an' breathe!"

Bannerman blanched. The newcomer was Black Bob Reardon, a desperado who had tried his hand at most things. Bannerman had arrested him four years earlier for armed robbery and he had served those four years in jail. Now he was pointing an accusing finger at the marshal. Bannerman determined to brazen it out. He had no other choice.

"You referrin' to me, mister?" he drawled.

"You bet I am, marshal," declared Reardon.

"Wa'al, you got the wrong man. I ain't no marshal, an' my name's Bannon, not Bannerman."

"Coincidence, though, the two names bein' so alike," murmured Daly.

"They ain't so alike," retorted Bannerman.

"They're enough alike to make me wonder," said Daly.

"Wonder what?"

"Whether yo're on the level."

"He ain't. I declare I ain't made no mistake. He's Bannerman okay," growled Black Bob Reardon.

Joe Daly glanced round at his four companions. They were all staring suspiciously at Bannerman. Bannerman suddenly pushed back his chair and leapt to his feet. He stood glaring at Black Bob Reardon.

"You callin' me a liar, mister?" he snarled, his hand hovering menacingly over the butt of his Colt Peacemaker.

However, before Reardon could reply, Daly intervened. He whipped out his Army Model Colt in a lightning-quick draw and aimed it across the table at Bannerman.

"Jest pull out yore gun nice 'n'

easy, an' lay it down on the table," he hissed.

Bannerman stared at the Major. Daly's pale blue eyes stared back at him cold and pitiless. There was no doubt that the outlaw would shoot him dead if he made the slightest false move. He had no option other than to do as he was bidden.

"Okay," he said. "If that's the way you want it." He slowly drew the Colt from its holster and laid it down on the table. "Seein' as you evidently don't trust me, guess I'll find me some other fellers to do business with," he added.

"No, I don't think so," said Daly. He beckoned the proprietor of the Lucky Chance from his position behind the bar. "You got a private room we can use, Marty?" he asked.

"Sure thing, Major," said the saloon-keeper, nervously rubbing his hands together. In common with most folks in Providence Flats, he was more than a little scared of the ex-Confederate officer.

He led the way into the rear quarters of the saloon and ushered them into a small, neatly furnished parlour. The first to enter was John Bannerman. He went reluctantly, with the barrel of Joe Daly's revolver digging into the small of his back. The last to enter was Black Bob Reardon.

Daly turned and surveyed the others.

"Thanks, Marty," he said. "You can go back to tendin' yore saloon. We won't be needin' you in here."

"No. 'Course not. I . . . I'll be g . . . goin', then, M . . . Major," stammered the saloon-keeper, and he hurried thankfully out of the room.

Daly then turned his attention to Black Bob Reardon.

"Guess we gotta thank you, Bob, for yore timely intervention. I'll be sure to buy you a few drinks later. But, for now, we got a li'l business to attend to, so if you don't mind . . ."

"But it was me who was arrested by . . ." began Reardon.

"I said we got business to attend to."

"I got an interest, too, Major. I wanta see that sonofabitch Bannerman dead. Hell, four years in Picton County Jail was no picnic!"

"Yeah, wa'al, me an' the boys, we don't like other folks stickin' their noses in on our business. No offence, Bob, but you ain't one of us. Therefore, I'd sure 'preciate it if 'n' you'd jest leave the marshal to us."

Daly spoke softly, almost gently, yet Reardon could sense the menace in his voice. Reardon shrugged his shoulders. He figured he could safely leave Bannerman to the Major's tender mercies.

"Okay. I'll be seein' you later," he growled, adding with a sudden grin, "To collect them drinks you spoke of."

Daly nodded and, when Black Bob Reardon had finally quit the parlour, he turned his attention to the marshal.

"Sit down," he said, pointing to one of two armchairs that stood on either side of the saloon-keeper's fireplace.

John Bannerman sat down. Despite the fire blazing in the grate, he felt distinctly chilly. Cold tendrils of naked fear clutched at his heart.

"Look here," he said, "you cain't be sure that feller ain't made a mistake. You spoke of searchin' me to see if I was carryin' a marshal's badge. Wa'al, why don't you do jest that?"

Daly smiled coldly and shook his head.

"Nope. I don't think we'll go to that trouble."

"Then, what . . . aaagh!"

Bannerman cried out as Daly suddenly lashed out and smashed him across the bridge of his nose with the barrel of his revolver. Once, twice, thrice Daly whipped the gun back and forth across the lawman's face. Blood gushed forth from Bannerman's nose as it was mercilessly mashed into a gory pulp. Then the revolver caught him in the mouth as he opened it to yell. He coughed up half a dozen teeth and a couple of mouthfuls of blood. But still

Daly continued to beat him about the face, reducing it to a misshapen crimson mass, the eyes blackened and closed, the nose a shattered lump of gore and bone, and the mouth a screaming bloody hole.

The screams could be heard quite clearly in the saloon. However, nobody was likely to come to Bannerman's aid. Providence Flats' denizens tended to mind their own business. Only the poker players were bothered by the screams, for Bannerman's yells were inclined to break their concentration. None of them, though, felt brave enough to protest.

Inside the saloon-keeper's parlour, Daly ignored Bannerman's screams and kept bashing away with the barrel of his gun, all the while repeating the same question.

"How did you git onto us, Bannerman?" he asked over and over again.

Three times the marshal lapsed into unconsciousness and three times he was brought round by the simple expedient of Bear throwing water in his face. It was the first occasion the Lucky Chance Saloon had been called upon to supply a customer with that particular commodity. And, as the saloon-keeper eyed Bannerman's bloodied features, he fervently hoped it would be the last.

It took almost an hour before Bannerman finally cracked. He was pretty darned tough, but every man has his breaking-point. Finally, he succumbed and mumbled through swollen, split lips, "Amy Scarlett . . . she . . . she described . . . you."

"Amy Scarlett? Who the heck is Amy Scarlett?" demanded Daly.

"On . . . on . . . the stage . . . 'tween Buffalo Casper," gasped Bannerman.

"The stage we held up a few days back? But there was only one woman aboard. A blonde. Is this Amy Scarlett a blonde?"

"Yes."

"In her mid-to-late thirties?"

"Yes."

Daly turned to face Bear. The huge, bearded outlaw stirred uncomfortably.

"Wa'al, Bear, whaddya say to that, huh? I told you to finish her off. Goddamit, I heard the shot!"

"Yeah. Sorry, Major, but I jest couldn't do it," growled Bear.

"Couldn't do it?"

"Nope. Never shot a woman before. Cain't explain it, but I found that I couldn't pull that trigger."

"But you did pull it!"

"Yeah. I pumped a shot into the floorboards of the stage. Hell, I figured she'd freeze to death for sure!"

"I'd've figured the same," interjected Elmer Judd.

"That's a point. How in tarnation did she survive?" rasped Daly.

"Feller . . . feller came along . . . took her . . . to stagin'-post . . . at Bighorn Springs," replied Bannerman brokenly.

"An' is she still there?" enquired the Major.

"N . . . nope."

"Then, jest where is she?"

"I . . . I dunno for sure."

"You want me to beat you up some more, Bannerman?" Daly's eyes glinted sadistically. "I'd like that," he hissed.

"No! No!" Bannerman croaked piteously through swollen, bloodied lips. He had endured as much pain as he could possibly take before he had finally broken. The thought of having to suffer more filled him with horror. "I . . . I'm tellin' you all I . . . I know," he muttered.

"Okay, so whaddya know?"

"Miss Scarlett . . . she was aimin' . . . to . . . to take the stage . . . from Casper to Laramie. Planned to . . . to catch the train there, y'see."

"The train?"

"For 'Frisco."

"She travellin' alone?"

"Yeah . . . that is . . . I ain't sure."

"You ain't sure?"

"Mebbe the feller who . . . who found her an' . . . an' took her to Bighorn Springs . . . mebbe he'll escort her as far as Laramie? I dunno 'bout that."

Daly fixed the marshal with an angry glare.

"Who is this feller?" he demanded.

"A Kentuckian . . . name of Stone. Jack Stone."

"Hell!" Daly whistled and turned to face the others. "You boys heard of Jack Stone, I guess?"

"Who ain't? Man's a livin' legend. They don' come no deadlier than Stone," said Eli Judd.

"Ain't he the feller who tamed Mallory, the roughest, toughest town in all Colorado?" added Elmer Judd glumly.

"He is," confirmed Daly.

"Wa'al, we sure don't wanta tangle with him," growled Bear.

"We may have to, if 'n' he's escortin' Miss Amy Scarlett to Laramie to catch that there train," said Daly.

"But why, Major? Why not let her go?" enquired Eli Judd.

"'Cause she's the one an' only person

who can put the finger on us."

"But if she's in 'Frisco . . . " began Bear.

"That ain't a million miles away."

"Nope, but it's still one helluva way from here."

"If the law wants her to give evidence agin' us, they'll bring her back quick enough." Daly smiled thinly and went on, "I tell you, boys, I ain't restin' till she's good 'n' dead!"

"The Major's right," declared Randy Wilkins. "While this woman lives, she's a danger to us all."

The other outlaws nodded grimly. They might have no wish to tangle with Jack Stone, but they preferred that prospect to the prospect of hanging. Besides, they did not know for sure that they would have to take on the famous Kentuckian gunfighter. It was possible that Amy Scarlett could be travelling alone.

"So, what do we do, Major?" asked Bear.

"We head for Casper an' try 'n' pick

up her trail," said Daly.

"What about the marshal here? We cain't jest leave him," said Wilkins.

"Nope." Daly turned to Bear. "Drag him outside, to the rear of the saloon, an' shoot him. An', this time, make no mistake," he rasped.

"Sure thing, Major," said Bear.

"I'll give you a hand," said Elmer Judd.

Between the pair of them, they dragged the softly moaning, semi-conscious marshal out of the parlour and along a short, dingy passage. Judd threw open the door at its far end, and yellow light spilled out to illuminate the snow-covered back yard of the Lucky Chance. Crates of empty whiskey bottles and a number of beer-barrels, some full and some empty, were stacked in the yard. They were situated to one side of the door, while an ancient, dilapidated cart stood directly in front of it. The two outlaws heaved Bannerman through the doorway and pushed him in the direction of the cart.

He caught hold of it to prevent himself from falling and swivelled round to face his would-be killers.

"This ain't such a good move, y'know," he gasped. "If you think about it, you'll soon . . ."

But Bannerman's words were drowned in the roar of gunfire, as Elmer Judd and Bear drew their Remingtons from their holsters and emptied them into him. He was thrown backwards against the cart, the hail of bullets ripping through flesh, muscle and bone and exiting out of his back. A last, piteous cry escaped his bloodied lips and he slid slowly down the side of the cart, to lie silent in the snow. Bear strolled across and peered down at Bannerman's lifeless, bullet-ridden corpse.

"Wa'al, the Major cain't say I failed to obey his orders this time," muttered the giant.

6

JAMIESON'S HOTEL was a decent enough hotel, exactly as Doc Norris had promised. One of only three in the small prairie town of Casper, it was easily the best. Clean, comfortable and as warm as any place could be during that chill, sub-zero winter, it provided Amy Scarlett and Jack Stone with reasonable accommodation while they awaited the arrival of the Wells Fargo stagecoach.

As they sat in the hotel dining-room on their first night in town, enjoying a quiet supper together, Amy determined to lay out a few ground rules.

"One thing we gotta git clear, Mr Stone," she began.

"Jack. Call me Jack. Hell, if we're gonna be together for the next few days . . . "That's what I wanta talk about."

"Oh, yeah?"

"Yup. What we've got here is a business arrangement."

"Yo're payin' my expenses, sure. But I don't see . . ."

"I 'preciate you waitin' here in Casper with me, Jack. But I don't want you to git any wrong ideas."

"'Bout you an' me?" Stone grinned.

"That's right. Okay, so I'm a saloon girl turned saloon-owner, an' have known one helluva lot of men in my time. But I'm aimin' to change all that. When I git to 'Frisco an' buy me a high-class dress shop, I'm gonna settle down an' become a most respectable an' highly respected member of society."

"Most commendable, Amy . . . er . . . I may call you Amy, I s'pose?" said the Kentuckian.

"Yes, you may, Jack. But you gotta understand that we're jest friends an' nothin' more. I didn't rent us a coupla rooms simply for the look of the thing," explained the blonde.

"I know you didn't," said Stone.

"You do?" Amy gazed at her companion in surprise.

"Sure. After what you've been through, you ain't gonna wanta share a bed with a man for some li'l time to come, I guess."

"It ain't that I don't find you attractive, Jack." Amy smiled relievedly. She had not imagined that the big, tough-looking Kentuckian would be so sensitive to her feelings. "But it's as you say. The thought of sharin' my bed with a man, any man, is . . . is kinda repugnant to me."

"Wa'al, I'll respect yore wishes on that score. You can depend on that," said Stone.

The Kentuckian spoke with utter sincerity. He found the blonde to be an attractive and stimulating companion, and would quite happily have jumped into bed with her. But he was not a man to force himself on any woman, particularly not one who had suffered the vile experiences which Amy Scarlett had so recently endured.

Thus Amy's ground rules were laid and, during the days that followed, though her relationship with Jack Stone naturally developed and flourished, it remained purely platonic.

Stone, for his part, made no attempt to breach Amy's rules. He thoroughly enjoyed her day-time company and gallantly put up with the night-time embargo.

* * *

The arrival of the stagecoach on a bitter winter's morning was greeted by both with a sense of relief. Amy was anxious to reach Laramie and, from there, set forth on the final leg of her journey to 'Frisco, while Stone was beginning to find the inactivity of the last few days rather tedious.

However, the stage did not set out again immediately, for the horses needed to be changed at the stage line depot. This afforded the passengers an opportunity to slip into Jamieson's Hotel and warm themselves with lashings of coffee and a good, hot meal. The driver and the shotgun guard, meantime, moseyed on over to the Silver Spurs Saloon, where they proposed to breakfast on pork and beans and a few hefty snorts of whiskey. It was there that Jack Stone found them.

"Howdy, boys," he said genially. "May I join you?"

"Help yoreself," said the driver.

"Thanks."

Stone pulled up a chair and sat down at their table. He offered them a drink from the bottle which he had brought across from the bar. This they accepted with alacrity.

"A safe journey to Laramie!" proposed Stone, raising his glass.

"A safe journey!" repeated the two Wells Fargo men, whereupon all three tossed back the whiskey.

"Let me introduce myself," said Stone.

"You don't have to. Yo're Jack Stone,

ain't you?" said the driver.

Stone smiled wryly. He sometimes wished he was less well-known. Being famous sure didn't make for a quiet life. He nodded.

"Spent a few days in Tombstone when you was deppity marshal there," explained the driver.

"So, you know I'm on the level," said Stone.

"Guess so."

"Would you mind, therefore, if I was to ride along with you as far as Laramie?"

"You want a seat on the coach?" asked the driver.

Stone shook his head.

"Nope. I propose ridin' alongside, on my hoss. If that's okay with you fellers?" he drawled.

"Sure. We'll be glad to have you along," said the driver.

"That's right," agreed the guard. Then, he stared hard at the Kentuckian and asked curiously, "Any reason why you wanta ride alongside us, Mr Stone?

You'd be a darned sight quicker ridin' on yore own."

"I know that," said Stone. "But I've been asked by one of yore passengers, Miss Amy Scarlett, if I'd accompany her on the ride to Laramie. She's a mite nervous 'bout travellin' on a stage since that last hold-up by them notorious Wyomin' Phantoms. Y'see, she was the sole survivor."

"Oh, yeah!" The driver nodded. "I heard 'bout that. Reckon the murderin' varmints slipped up there."

"They sure did. Now, at last, there's someone still alive who can bear witness agin' them. Which is another reason why Miss Scarlett's nervous."

"But the outlaws don't know she's still alive, do they?" muttered the guard.

"I don't b'lieve so. But, anyways, Miss Scarlett reckons she'll feel happier if I accompany the stage."

"Wa'al, I can understand that," said the driver.

At this point, the bartender appeared

on the scene, bearing two large platefuls of pork and beans, which he slapped down on the table in front of the two Wells Fargo men. Stone smiled and replenished their glasses. Thereupon, he rose to his feet.

"I'll let you enjoy yore meal," he said. "Be seein' you both later."

"Yeah, see you later, Mr Stone," replied the driver.

Stone threw back the remains of his whiskey, corked the bottle and made his way slowly out through the batwing doors. He paused on the stoop outside the saloon and then turned left and headed for the livery stables.

It was half an hour later when the passengers emerged from the hotel and began to climb into the stagecoach. Two businessmen from the East Coast, a mining engineer, and an elderly couple on their way to visit their daughter in Cheyenne, all preceded Amy Scarlett. She paused for a moment, her foot on the step, and glanced towards Stone, who was already mounted and holding in his gelding prior to their setting forth. He raised his Stetson and smiled at the blonde.

"Don't worry Amy," he cried. "Yore journey to Laramie is gonna be long, tedious, borin' an' entirely uneventful."

"I do hope so!" replied Amy, whereupon she smiled nervously and clambered into the coach.

Immediately the door had slammed shut behind Amy, the driver cracked his whip and the stagecoach rattled off down Main Street. A few paces behind it trotted the Kentuckian on his bay gelding. He peered up into the sky. It was deep blue and crystal-clear. The day might be bitterly cold, he mused, but at least there was no sign of snow in the air. He urged his steed forward and, as he passed beyond the town limits, drew level with the stagecoach.

★ ★ ★

Major Joe Daly and his gang rode into Casper shortly before noon, two hours after the departure of the stagecoach carrying Amy Scarlett on her way to Laramie. They dismounted outside the Silver Spurs Saloon, hitched their horses to the rail and trooped up the steps onto the stoop. Before they could proceed into the saloon, however, Daly halted in front of the batwing doors and held up his hand. He turned to face the others.

"Okay, boys, what's needed now are a few discreet enquiries. I reckon me 'n' Elmer had best make 'em. The rest of you take it easy with the drinkin' an' see you don't git into no fights. I want us to ease in an' outta this town jest as though we ain't never been here. Got it?" Daly eyed each of the outlaws in turn. "Got it?" he repeated.

"Yeah, we got it, Major. You can depend on us," said Bear.

"Okay; wa'al, I'll see you boys later." Daly turned to Elmer Judd. "Elmer," he said, "you take the roomin'-houses. There's 'bout six or seven. I'll take the hotels."

"But what . . . what am I to say, Major?" asked Judd.

Daly thought for a few moments before replying.

"Say yo're lookin' for yore sister, to tell her yore pa's died," he said. "You can explain that you'd heard she was stoppin' over in Casper while waitin' for the stage to take her to Laramie."

"Okay, Major."

"An' mention that you'd also heard she was travellin' with a male companion, a Kentuckian," said Daly. "For we wanta know whether or not we've gotta deal with that sonofabitch, Stone."

"An' s'pose I find Miss Scarlett? What then?"

"Don't go nowhere near her. Jest make some excuse to leave, an' hightail it back here to the Silver Spurs."

"But what kinda excuse can I make?"

"Say you've brought yore wife along, 'cause she'll be able to break the news of yore pa's death more gently than you could. Say yo're gonna fetch her."

Elmer Judd smiled. The Major

thought of everything.

"Right," he said.

"You've got all that?" quizzed Daly.

"I have."

"Wa'al, let's git goin."

The two men split up, Judd heading along the sidewalk towards the nearest of the town's rooming-houses, while Daly crossed the street and made straight for Jamieson's Hotel."

In the event, Daly emerged from the hotel two minutes later, a look of triumph on his face. He hailed Judd, who, at that moment, was about to knock on the door of the second rooming-house. Immediately, Judd abandoned his search and they both retraced their steps to the Silver Spurs Saloon.

When Joe Daly and Elmer Judd entered the saloon, they found the others sitting at a corner table, quietly drinking. There was a bottle of whiskey on the table and two clean glasses, which Bear promptly filled. The two men sat down and lifted the glasses.

They tossed back the red-eye in one gulp.

"Ah, that's better!" cried Daly, at the same time beating himself in an attempt to pound some warmth into his chilled body.

Although they were sitting only a few feet from one of the saloon's pot-bellied stoves, it was still as cold as charity inside the saloon. The most that could be said, was that they were protected from the bitter wind which whistled through the streets of the prairie town.

"Wa'al, did you find her?" enquired Randy Wilkins eagerly.

"We did. Leastways, the Major did," said Elmer Judd.

Joe Daly nodded.

"She was stayin' at Jamieson's Hotel. And so was Stone," he said.

"Hell! Cain't say I'm keen to tangle with him!" growled Bear.

"You leave Jack Stone to me. There ain't nobody I cain't outdraw," boasted Wilkins arrogantly.

Daly stared coldly at the black-clad youth.

"Don't be too sure," he rasped. "This feller Stone's a tough hombre, an' he's goddam fast with a gun. He ain't gonna be no easy meat."

"You said they was stayin' at Jamieson's Hotel. Does that mean they ain't there no more?" asked Eli Judd.

"That's right, Eli. They set out for Laramie 'bout two hours back," said Daly.

"On the stage?" enquired Bear.

"Miss Scarlett, she was on the stage. Stone, he was ridin' alongside," explained Daly.

"So, what now?" growled Bear.

"We pursue 'em. They're sure to stop-over for 'bout an hour at the stagin'-post at Brough's Ford. If 'n' they don't need to change horses, they'll still wanta warm up some an' git a li'l food inside 'em. Wa'al, I reckon we can reach Brough's Ford 'fore they set out agin."

"An' do we bust in an' shoot

everyone up, huh?" hissed Wilkins, a sadistic gleam in his eye.

"Nope. Our aim is to kill Miss Amy Scarlett so she cain't ever give evidence agin' us, right?"

"Right, Major."

"Then, that's all we're gonna do. I ain't plannin' to shoot up nobody else."

"What about Stone?" demanded Wilkins.

"I'm hopin' we can do this without havin' to take him on," said Daly.

"Wa'al, that suits me," said Elmer Judd.

"An' me," added his brother.

"An' jest how do you plan to avoid takin' on Stone?" enquired Bear.

"I'll explain when we catch up with the stage," said Daly. Then he grinned and, having tossed back a second whiskey, declared, "Okay, boys, if 'n' we are to make Brough's Ford in time to catch the stage, I guess we'd better lam outta here."

He promptly rose to his feet, and the

others hastily finished their whiskies and followed him out through the batwing doors into Casper's Main Street. A couple of minutes later, the five outlaws were galloping hell-for-leather out past the town limits and along the trail towards Laramie.

7

JACK STONE did not content himself with simply riding alongside the stagecoach. Although he had no real reason to suppose the Wyoming Phantoms were likely to strike, Stone, being a naturally cautious man, acted as if he did. Consequently, he rode up and down the trail, sometimes riding on ahead of the stage to check for any possible ambush, and sometimes dropping back to check that the stage was not being pursued.

Stone's caution paid off. The stage was a couple of miles short of Brough's Ford when he once again dropped back. He mounted a ridge and, from the cover of a tumble of boulders, narrowed his eyes and peered into the distance. At first he could see nothing but the seemingly endless vista of snow-covered prairie. Then, on the horizon, there appeared what looked like small clouds of white dust. Snow being kicked up by a bunch of galloping horses, he guessed. Stone concentrated his gaze. Finally, he could just make them out. Five tiny black specks. Were they pursuing the stagecoach or merely travelling in the same direction? Stone did not know, but he determined to take no chances. His instincts warned him that those five specks on the horizon spelt danger. And the Kentuckian was not a man to disregard his instincts. Too often in the past they had saved his life. He turned the gelding's head and set off after the stagecoach.

By the time Stone eventually caught up with it, it had reached Brough's Ford and was easing to a halt before the log cabin that served as bar-room and diner for anyone who cared to call, and as living quarters for the staging-post manager and his wife.

Stone had no sooner dismounted than the staging-post manager, a small, craggy, grey-haired fellow called Archie

Bean, threw open the door of the cabin and stepped outside.

"C'mon in, folks!" he cried. "My wife's got some real good beef stew cookin' away on the stove. Git some of that inside y'all, an' you'll soon warm up, I promise you."

The response to this invitation was instantaneous. The passengers tumbled out of the stagecoach, and, led by the mining engineer, hurried across the snow towards the cabin. Amy Scarlett had almost reached the doorway when the Kentuckian caught up with her and pulled her to one side. He waited until the others had disappeared inside the cabin. Then he broke the bad news.

"There was five of them so-called Wyomin' Phantoms, wasn't there?" he whispered.

"Yes. Why?" Amy stared wide-eyed at the Kentuckian. Her heart suddenly began to pound and she felt the chill fingers of fear claw at the pit of her stomach.

"'Cause we got five riders on our

trail," said Stone.

"What! You . . . you don't think that . . . ?" Amy left her question unsaid.

"I dunno. But I ain't takin' no chances. Reckon it'll take 'em 'bout an hour to reach Brough's Ford."

"So?"

"So, we have a chance." Stone smiled reassuringly at the blonde. "Don't worry, Amy, even if it is them goddam Phantoms, they ain't gonna catch you. No, sirree!"

"But the stage won't be leavin' for 'bout an hour. An', anyways, supposin' it does leave 'fore they git here, they'll soon catch up with it!" cried Amy.

"I've already thought of that, an' I've got me a plan. Mebbe 'tain't entirely foolproof, but I figure it'll work," drawled Stone.

Amy stared at the Kentuckian and prayed that he was right. If it didn't work, the consequences would be too horrific for her even to contemplate.

"What is yore plan?" she asked nervously.

Again Stone smiled. And then he told her.

★ ★ ★

Joe Daly and his gang veered off the trail and rode up onto the bluff that overlooked Brough's Ford. Leaving the Judd brothers to take care of the horses, Daly, Bear and Randy Wilkins walked up to the edge of the bluff and peered down at the staging-post. Daly surveyed the cabin, the corral, the stables and the few tumbledown outhouses. A thin stream of smoke snaked up from the cabin's chimney, to be quickly dispersed by the wintry wind. Daly shivered. It was hellish cold up on that snowy, windswept bluff. He longed to enter the cabin and warm himself in front of Archie Bean's fire. But that wasn't part of his scheme. He concentrated his gaze on the stagecoach standing outside Archie Bean's cabin, and a grim smile flickered across his bold, handsome features. He fingered the sabre scar on his cheek and turned to Bear.

"Guess Miss Scarlett is inside that there cabin with the rest of the folks off the stage," he muttered.

"Guess so, Major," replied Bear.

"So, why don't we go down 'n' jest bust in an' gun 'em all down?" enquired Randy Wilkins, his eyes gleaming excitedly at the thought of all that killing.

Daly eyed the psychopathic youth coldly and shook his head.

"No, Randy, I already told you," he growled. "We're here for one purpose only . . . to silence Miss Amy Scarlett."

"But, if she's down there with them others . . . " began Wilkins.

"When she leaves the cabin to board the stage, we pick her off from up here," explained Daly.

"That'll be one helluva difficult shot."

"Not with Bear's buffalo-gun, it won't."

Randy Wilkins considered this. Then

he smiled. The Major was right. It would be dead easy using the Sharps rifle with its telescopic sights.

Bear wasn't smiling, though.

"Hell, Major!" he exclaimed. "You want me to shoot her?"

Again Daly shook his head.

"Nope. You got this hang-up 'bout shootin' women. So, we'll leave it to Randy here. He's happy to shoot anyone an' anythin' that moves. Ain't that right, Randy?"

"You bet, Major. So, do I git to use Bear's buffalo-gun?"

"That okay by you, Bear?" murmured Daly.

He knew that Bear didn't like anyone other than himself to handle the Sharps rifle. But Bear had little choice, unless he took it upon himself to shoot Amy Scarlett. The giant reflected for a moment or two and then reluctantly nodded his huge, shaggy head.

"I'll go fetch it," he said, and he retreated to where the Judd brothers stood with the horses.

Meantime, Daly fixed Randy Wilkins with a fierce, penetrating stare.

"I don't want no massacre, Randy," he said. "You pick off Miss Scarlett, an' only Miss Scarlett. Then we drop down off this bluff an' high-tail it back to Providence Flats. Is that clear?"

"I don't understand, Major. I could easily shoot up the other passengers an' then . . ."

"You might not git 'em all. An', if 'n' they barricade theirselves in that stagin'-post cabin, we could have some trouble prisin' 'em out. No, like I said, we're here for one reason an' one reason only, to prevent Amy Scarlett from ever bearin' witness agin' us. Let's jest do what we came to do an' then lam outta here." Daly continued to stare hard and long at the black-clad youth. "That's an order, Randy," he said.

Wilkins dropped his gaze. He feared the Major as he feared no other man. He knew that, should he start shooting Amy Scarlett's fellow-passengers, Joe

Daly would plug him for sure. His orders were not to be disobeyed.

"Okay," he muttered. "I shoot Miss Amy Scarlett an' nobody else."

"That's right, kid," said Daly.

As the Major spoke, so Bear returned bearing the buffalo-gun. He handed it to Wilkins and, without a word, crouched down in the snow beside the youth. The three gunslingers waited expectantly, while a few yards behind them, the Judd brothers tended to the horses and did what they could to stop themselves from freezing to death.

Their wait was fortunately of short duration. Randy Wilkins had lined up the target area between the cabin and the stagecoach, and adjusted the rifle's telescopic sights. And he had taken aim at an imaginary Amy Scarlett. It was as he turned to Joe Daly and Bear to whisper, "It's gonna be plumb easy. Like shootin' bottles at a fair," that the door of the cabin suddenly swung open.

The first person to emerge was the

stagecoach driver. He was immediately followed by the guard, who, while the driver clambered up onto the box, threw open the stagecoach door and proceeded to help the elderly couple climb inside. The two East Coast businessmen and the mining engineer had seemingly struck up a friendship over dinner, for they came out of the cabin together. They hurried after the others and jumped into the coach, whereupon the guard slammed shut the door and quickly joined the driver on the box. Then, the driver flicked the reins and the stagecoach slowly moved off.

★ ★ ★

As the stage swung southwards down the trail, the driver breathed a huge sigh of relief.

"Wa'al," he said, "I guess Stone was right when he advised us to keep quiet 'bout what he'd told us."

"Yeah," said the guard. "If we'd told

the passengers that we was expectin' them murderin' Wyomin' Phantoms to jump us, they'd have panicked for sure."

"An' then the bastards would've known somethin' was up an' they'd certainly have jumped us."

"You reckon they was up there on that bluff overlookin' Brough's Ford?"

"I do. Sittin' there, jest like Stone figured, waitin' to pick off Miss Scarlett."

"Only she didn't put in an appearance."

"Nope. That must've puzzled 'em some."

"Whaddya reckon they'll do now? Come after us?"

The driver shook his head.

"Nope. I reckon we're in the clear," he said. "They'll most likely send one of their number down to the stagin'-post to question Archie Bean 'bout Miss Scarlett's non-appearance."

"But he only knows what Stone told him. An' that sure wasn't the truth," said the guard.

"Exactly."

"You think those sonsofbitchs'll believe Archie an' head off on the wrong trail?"

"Dunno. But I hope so, for Stone's an' Miss Scarlett's sakes."

So saying, the driver leant forward and urged the horses to an even greater speed.

★ ★ ★

Meantime, back on top of the bluff, Joe Daly was quietly cursing. Bear eyed him uneasily. He knew he was to blame for the fact that Amy Scarlett was still alive.

"D'you think the woman's still inside the cabin?" he mumbled.

"Or mebbe she never got outta the stage? Mebbe she stayed aboard while the others . . . " began Randy Wilkins.

"Is that likely? Why the heck would she sit out there freezin' when there was food 'n' warmth to be had inside the cabin? Nope. There's jest two possibilities. Either Bear's right an' she's still in the cabin, or she's left, but not on the stage," said Daly.

"But how could she have left?" asked the youth, rising and handing the unused buffalo-gun back to its owner.

"On horseback; that's how," snarled Daly.

"But . . ."

"The Kentuckian, Jack Stone, was s'posed to be accompanyin' the stage. Wa'al, where is he?"

"Goddam it, Major, that's right! We ain't seen him an' there is no sign of his hoss hitched up outside the cabin. You reckon he an' she . . . ?"

"I do, Randy."

"Then, let's git down there an' find out!" cried the youth.

"We ain't goin' nowheres. Not yet." Daly turned and summoned Elmer Judd from where he stood with the horses. "Elmer," he said, "I want you to ride down there an' find out what's happened to Miss Scarlett. You can use the same story you used back in Casper. An' if, as I suspect, yo're told she an' Stone left on horseback, ask when an' in which direction they was headed. Then check outside to make sure you've been told the truth. An', when you've done that, report back here."

"Okay, Major, will do," said Elmer Judd.

The others watched him ride off. They waited impatiently while he cantered down towards the staging-post. Then he disappeared inside the cabin and they continued to wait.

It was some fifteen minutes later when he rejoined them on the bluff, and they could tell, from the scowl that darkened his ugly, bearded features, that he did not bring good news.

"Wa'al?" growled Joe Daly.

"It's like you figured, Major," said Elmer Judd. And he went on to relate what Archie Bean had told him.

It seemed that, upon their arrival in the cabin, Jack Stone and Amy

Scarlett had approached Archie Bean and asked if they could buy one of his horses. They had explained that Amy had changed her mind and no longer wanted to go to Laramie. Instead, she intended to ride up through the mountains to Rock Springs. A deal had been struck and a suitably docile horse had been found for Amy, who, it appeared, was no horsewoman. By Archie Bean's reckoning, they had been gone an hour or more.

Again Joe Daly quietly cursed.

"Gee, Major, why in hell would she wanta go to Rock Springs?" enquired Randy Wilkins. "I thought that marshal told us she was aimin' to catch a train to 'Frisco?"

"Yeah. She'd need to go to Laramie to catch that," commented Eli Judd.

"Yes." Daly glared at the elder Judd brother. "Did you check to see if you had been told the truth?" he demanded.

"Sure did, Major," said Elmer Judd. "There's two sets of hoof-marks in the snow. Both lead off from the back of the stagin'-post. An' they point west, up towards the mountain country 'tween here an' Rock Springs."

"Then, let's mount up an' follow that trail. Providin' it don't snow no more, we should be able to see their tracks easy enough," said Daly.

"You reckon they are headin' for Rock Springs, then, Major?" asked Bear.

"Nope. I reckon they're headin' for Laramie," replied Daly.

Randy Wilkins stared in bewilderment at the Major.

"But why in hell should they strike off on their own? If Miss Scarlett ain't no horsewoman, why didn't she jest continue to travel there by stage?" he demanded.

"Mebbe Stone somehow found out that we was after 'em," suggested Daly.

"But how . . . ?" began Bear.

"I dunno, an' I don't care. All I'm interested in is catchin' up with 'em. So, let's go!" cried the outlaw chief.

He threw himself into the saddle and the others hastily followed. Then, with one last glance down at the staging-post, Daly turned his gelding's head and set off westward.

Soon they picked up the tracks of their quarry. Ahead of them lay the rugged terrain that began to the west of Brough's Ford, encompassing hill country, tracts of forest and ravines, and eventually rising up into the distant Medicine Bow Range. It was going to be a long, hard ride.

8

THE Kentuckian glanced anxiously at his blonde companion. She had spoken the truth when she said she was no horsewoman. Consequently, their progress up into the mountains had been unconscionably slow. The grey mare, which Archie Bean had provided, was as docile as any horse in Wyoming and therefore suited Amy well enough. But her natural sluggishness combined with Amy's inexperience as a rider, kept them travelling at a pace which Stone feared would prove much too slow. They had, he reckoned, approximately one hour's start over their pursuers. At their present rate of progress, that was nowhere near enough.

Stone had decided to cut out from Brough's Ford before the outlaws arrived on the scene, since to have done otherwise would have been to court disaster, not only for Amy and himself, but also for Amy's fellow-travellers. This way, they had a chance to out-run their pursuers. At least, that had been Stone's original plan. Now he was not so sure. Unless Amy could spur the mare to greater effort, they would have to rely solely upon hood-winking the outlaws.

The Kentuckian had told Archie Bean that Amy had changed her mind about heading for Laramie and, instead, intended going through the mountains to Rock Springs. This was not true. They were, in fact, still aiming to reach Laramie, and were pursuing a course through the mountains, a course which ran parallel to the main trail between Casper and Laramie. This deception had been intended to throw the Wyoming Phantoms off their trail. Stone realised, however, that this rather transparent deceit was unlikely to fool the outlaws. For one thing, there was no way he could cover their tracks. A light fall of snow was what was needed to do that. Yet Stone had no wish that they should endure a full-scale blizzard. Indeed, he wondered whether Amy, after all she had been through, could survive such an ordeal. He glanced upwards. The sky was a vivid blue and completely clear of any clouds. The air was crisp and clean. Neither shower nor blizzard was likely.

"How are you doin', Amy?" he asked solicitously.

"Fine. Jest fine," replied the blonde, although, in truth, she was very weary.

Unused to riding and still fairly weak from her recent terrible experience and subsequent illness, Amy wondered whether she could manage the long ride to Laramie. Certainly, she would need to make frequent halts. But if they did that . . .

"Is there any sign of our pursuers?" she asked anxiously.

Stone turned in the saddle and peered back towards Brough's Ford. Hillside and gully, forest and stream lay between him and the Wells Fargo staging-post. Of the five horsemen there was no sign. They could, however, be out of sight anywhere back there in the fifteen miles they had covered since leaving Brough's Ford.

"I cain't see 'em," he said.

"Do you think mebbe we've thrown 'em off our trail?" said Amy.

"I doubt it."

"So, we jest keep goin', an' hope to stay ahead of 'em, huh?"

"Yup."

Stone had no wish to feed Amy with false hopes. He wanted her to keep going just as fast as the grey mare could carry her.

Ahead of them lay a narrow gully through which ran a winding, meandering stream. The stream was covered in a thin layer of ice, while huge icicles hung from the boulders that jutted out from both sides of the gully. It was into this windswept, wintry passage that the Kentuckian urged his gelding. He trotted alongside the stream, with Amy following a few yards behind him.

They had proceeded about a quarter of a mile into the gully when suddenly, upon turning a bend, Stone reined in the gelding and raised his hand. Amy promptly pulled up the grey mare.

"What is it?" she whispered.

Stone pointed towards the far end of the defile. A lone rider was slowly entering it. Amy gasped. She was alarmed to observe that he was a buckskin-clad Indian brave mounted upon a small, coal-black racing pony. Tall and lean, he wore three eagle feathers in his head-dress and carried a bow and a quiver of arrows. His only other weapon was the hunting-knife which he wore in his belt.

However, it was not only the Indian that had caught Stone's eye. Crouching on a ledge near the entrance to the gully was a huge mountain lion. This ledge was situated some eight feet from the ground and directly above the path being taken by the Indian.

Stone knew that mountain lions rarely attacked human beings, preferring easier prey such as deer, buck rabbits and other small mammals. But, reduced almost to starvation by the bitter winter, the lion was evidently desperate enough to attack the Indian. And the Indian, unaware of his danger, was likely to prove easy meat for the ferocious beast. He rode on, quite oblivious to the presence of the mountain lion, until he was immediately beneath the ledge.

As the lion growled and sprang, so Jack Stone whipped the Winchester from his saddleboot, aimed and fired. The first shot struck the animal in the shoulder and hurled it backwards, so that it missed its mark and landed with a thud on the ground, a couple of feet to the left of the Indian. Immediately, the Indian's pony reared, presenting Stone with the opportunity to lease off another shot. The second bullet struck the lion in the chest, killing it outright.

The Indian brave struggled to

control the rearing pony and eventually succeeded in calming the beast. Then he glanced from the lifeless mountain lion down the gully towards the Kentuckian. A grim smile split his dark, hawk-like visage and he raised a hand in greeting.

Stone trotted forward, followed by an apprehensive Amy Scarlett. She had had little contact with the redskins and, like many white folk, was unfairly prejudiced against them, regarding them as murdering, scalp-hunting savages. She was reassured somewhat, though, when Stone addressed the man in his native tongue and the Indian responded in a friendly manner. The two men spoke together for a few minutes and then passed on, Stone and Amy continuing southwards, while the Indian headed deeper into the gully.

"I didn't know you could speak their language," said Amy.

"I speak some of their dialects," replied Stone.

"And which dialect was that?"

"Cheyenne."

"I thought the Cheyenne nation was confined to the reservation?"

"Yo're right. They are s'posed to be confined to reservation lands, but not all of 'em obey the law."

"Yeah, I know. There are those who have formed theirselves into renegade bands an' go around terrorisin' homesteaders an' ranchers an' . . ."

"That feller wasn't no renegade, if that's what yo're thinkin'. No sirree, he jest wants to continue in the old ways."

"The old ways?"

"Huntin', fishin', an' jest ridin' where he goddam pleases."

"Must be a kinda lonely existence, though."

"Guess so. But preferable to bein' cooped up on a reservation. Leastways, if 'n' yo're a free spirit, it is."

"Yo're somethin' of a free spirit yoreself, ain't you, Jack?"

"S'pose I am."

"Was that all you talked about

". . . him continuin' his old way of life?"

"Mostly, though he wanted to know what we was doin' out here in this wilderness."

"An' did you tell him?"

"I said we was headin' for Laramie."

"He must've wondered why in tarnation we hadn't stuck to the main trail."

"Yeah."

"But he didn't ask?"

"Nope. Too polite, I guess."

"Polite, huh? I never figured I'd hear anyone call an Injun polite. Savage, treacherous, murderin', yeah. But polite . . ."

"Like most white folks, you don't know nothin' 'bout the Injun, 'ceptin' what you've been told. Wa'al, don't go believin' everythin' that's said 'bout the redman. He ain't jest the simple, painted savage that the Government would have us believe. Cheyenne, Pawnee, Sioux, Crow, they're all different." Stone smiled and then murmured apologetically, "But, hell, I ain't got no business lecturin' you. No business at all."

"That's okay." Amy smiled back at him. "I'm findin' it mighty interestin', Jack," she said.

"Yeah, wa'al, I'll finish the lecture another time," replied the Kentuckian. "For the moment, let's jest keep goin'. We've got one helluva lot of miles ahead of us."

He glanced back along the gully. The Cheyenne had vanished. He tightened his grip on the reins and urged his bay gelding into a canter, and Amy gamely followed.

For the next couple of hours, they rode on through deep forests, over low hills and along narrow ravines, only too aware that their pursuers must be hot on their trail.

Dusk was beginning to fall when Amy finally broke the silence.

"Jack!" she cried. "I cain't go on much longer. I'm plumb tuckered out."

Stone turned in the saddle.

"Another hour an' it'll be dark. We'll find some place to hole up for the night," he said.

"What about them murderin' coyotes back there on our trail?"

"They cain't see in the dark no more than we can. They'll have to lay up some place overnight, too."

"I see. Then, mebbe, when I've rested for an hour or two, we could push on? That'd give us a few hours' start on 'em."

Stone considered the blonde. She was pretty near exhausted and yet she was willing to contemplate recommencing their ride after only the briefest of halts. She was some tough lady!

"Nope," he said. "Too dangerous. If one of our hosses was to stumble in the dark an' break its leg, we'd be done for. We'll start out again at first light, not before."

"But those sonsofabitch . . . ."

"We had an hour's start on 'em. Mebbe we're still an hour ahead of 'em."

Stone did not believe this. If those five riders he had seen heading towards Brough's Ford were indeed the Wyoming Phantoms, then he reckoned they would have made up most, if not all, of that hour by now.

In the event, three quarters of an hour later, Stone found a large cave cut into the rock-face, half-way down a winding, boulder-strewn ravine. It was large enough to hold Amy and himself, and their two horses. He led the way into the cave and promptly dismounted. Then he helped Amy down from her saddle.

"This'll do," he said. "We can light a fire in here an' it won't be seen from outside."

Amy nodded. She was chilled to the bone and the thought of spending the night without the comfort that a fire would provide had filled her with unutterable gloom. Now she brightened up.

There was an abundance of sticks and twigs to be found in the ravine and Stone soon had a fire blazing. With blankets wrapped tightly round their shoulders, he and Amy sat round the fire and enjoyed their frugal supper. It consisted of mugs of hot coffee and a little hardtack which Stone had obtained from Archie Bean. It hardly matched up to some of the sumptuous meals Amy had enjoyed while in her prime in New Orleans. Nor did it compare with those she had had in more recent times as joint owner of the Jack of Hearts Saloon in Sheridan. But just then Amy, shivering with cold, and exhausted and famished, regarded it as about the best supper she had ever eaten.

When they had finished their meal, Stone piled some more wood on the fire and then lay down on the cave floor to sleep.

"You . . . you ain't proposin' to sleep, are you?" exclaimed Amy in alarm.

"Sure. Why not?" asked the Kentuckian.

"But if them Wyomin' Phantoms are on our trail, they could follow our tracks in here an' . . ."

"Follow our tracks? In the dark? You gotta be kiddin'. 'Sides, this is pretty wild country an' no place to go stumblin' around at night. We don't need to worry 'bout them till the sun rises tomorrow. An' we'll be outta here at first light."

Amy glanced over her shoulder towards the entrance to the cave. By now it was pitch dark outside. She snuggled down beside the fire and prayed that the Kentuckian was right.

* * *

The trail was easy to follow. Joe Daly grinned. Unless it snowed and so obliterated the tracks of the two horses, sooner or later he would be sure to catch up with Miss Amy Scarlett and her protector. Then he and his boys would have themselves some fun. And this time there would be no mistake.

Amy and Stone would surely die.

He peered round at his band of desperadoes. All of them were tough, straight-shooting, cold-blooded killers. He reckoned they would be more than a match for Jack Stone. Not that he underestimated Stone. The Kentuckian was a living legend and would be certain to give them a hard fight.

"Okay, boys," he said, "I reckon we best look for somewhere to camp."

"But we cain't be far behind Stone an' the woman! Another hour an' we must catch 'em up, sure as hell!" said Randy Wilkins, his cruel blue eyes glistening as he visualised violating and then pumping bullets into Amy's voluptuous white body.

"It's gittin' dark. How'd you propose we follow their tracks, huh? You got night-vision like the cougar an' the coyote?" rasped Daly.

"No, Major, I guess not," conceded the youth.

"Then, we do as I say. We hole up for the night an' continue our pursuit at daybreak," said Daly.

"Major's right," growled Bear. "We press on, we could lose their tracks altogether. An' we ain't rightly sure jest where they're headin'."

"That feller at the stagin'-post said they was makin' for Rock Springs," said Elmer Judd. "But, so far, it'd seem they was makin' for Laramie, like the Major reckoned."

"Wa'al, we'll find out for sure in the mornin'," said Daly, and he swung out of the saddle and led his horse into the shelter of a stand of cottonwoods.

The others followed, and soon they had their horses tethered and a campfire blazing. While the rest sat round it talking and drinking coffee, Randy Wilkins walked a little way off and peered anxiously along the trail. He was eager to catch up with Amy and Stone, for he wanted to test himself against the famous Kentuckian gunfighter. His fellow-outlaws might have no wish to tangle with Stone, but the youth did not share their fears. A psychopath who delighted in killing, he had supreme confidence in his ability to out-shoot anyone who stood against him. He continued to peer through the deepening gloom. How close were they to their quarry, he wondered. In fact, Stone and the blonde were holed up less than half a mile further along the trail. The chase was almost over.

9

FIRST light found Jack Stone awake and ready to move out. But Amy Scarlett was in no condition to endure another hard day's ride across the frozen Wyoming landscape. She awoke from a few hours' broken sleep, cold, weary and frightened. She had still not fully recovered from her recent ordeal and the journey from Brough's Ford through rugged mountain country had taken its toll on her slender physical resources.

"I . . . I don't know if I can make the ride to Laramie," she confessed tearfully.

"We can take it a li'l easier, mebbe," said Stone.

He cast a sympathetic, yet watchful eye at the blonde and at once realised that she was very close to the limits of her endurance.

"But if 'n' we do that, those murderin' skunks'll catch us for sure," murmured Amy.

This was the truth and the Kentuckian saw that there was no point in denying it.

Yeah, Amy, guess yo're right 'bout that," he drawled.

"So, what can we do?" Amy shook her head sadly and sighed. You'd best leave me. There ain't no point in us both gittin' killed," she said.

"Wa'al, we ain't one hundred per cent certain that those five riders I saw headin' for Brough's Ford are the same five that held up yore stage."

"No, but . . . "

"So, it seems to me that, before we talk of me leavin' you, or of any other plan for that matter, it might be a good idea if I was to ride back along the trail a li'l ways, jest to see if we are in fact bein' pursued."

"Yes, all right. But . . . but be careful, Jack."

"You bet I will."

Stone smiled at the blonde and swung easily into the saddle. Then, leaving Amy and her grey mare in the cave, he trotted off, back down the ravine in the direction from which they had come.

The Kentuckian rode cautiously, avoiding, as far as possible, the various patches of scree and loose pebbles, and trusting to the snow to deaden the sound of his gelding's hooves. In this manner, he proceeded to the mouth of the ravine. Here he halted and gazed across a stretch of open scrubland towards a small stand of cottonwoods. And there, moving about among the trees, he saw them.

Stone narrowed his eyes and gazed intently at the men busily saddling up prior to moving out. There were indeed five of them. He concentrated his gaze. A grim smile played upon his lips. There was now no doubt in his mind that Amy and he were being pursued by the infamous Wyoming Phantoms, for the five matched exactly the descriptions given by Amy to US Marshal John Bannerman. He reached for his Winchester and pulled it clear of his saddleboot.

Stone's plan was a simple one. He intended to bushwhack the outlaws. There was no question that the outlaws' aim was to catch up with Amy and himself and kill the pair of them. Stone, therefore, had no compunction about shooting down his pursuers without warning. To survive against these ruthless, coldblooded killers he had to be as ruthless and coldblooded as they were.

He dismounted and slipped behind a large boulder, which apparently had been dislodged from the cliffs on the right-hand side of the ravine. Then he jammed the stock of the rifle hard into his right shoulder and took careful aim.

Eli Judd had the misfortune of being Stone's first chosen target. The rifle-shot cracked across the open scrub and the slug hit him in the chest, knocking him backwards into the arms of his brother. Three further shots shattered the silence of the wintry dawn. Of these, one whipped Randy Wilkins' black Stetson off his head, another struck Elmer Judd in the shoulder and the third buried itself in Eli Judd's belly.

The reaction of the outlaws was both swift and predictable. They dived down into the cover of the cottonwoods and hurriedly returned fire.

"How bad's Eli hit?" demanded Joe Daly, as he peered towards the ravine, desperately trying to locate the position of their attacker.

"Real bad. He's . . . hell . . . he's dead! The bastard's killed him!" cried Elmer Judd, clutching at his wounded shoulder.

"It's jest as I guessed," rasped Daly. "Jack Stone's tumbled to the fact we're on his trail. An' he's decided to git us 'fore we can git to him."

"He didn't give Eli a chance!" exclaimed Elmer Judd.

"Nope."

"The mean sonofabitch! Wa'al, nobody kills a Judd an' gits away with it!"

So saying, Elmer Judd struggled to his feet, rammed his Remington back into its holster and, pulling his .30 Spencer rifle from his saddleboot, began to stagger recklessly across the scrubland towards the ravine.

"Don't be a fool, Elmer! Whaddya think yo're doin'?" cried Daly.

But Elmer Judd took no notice of him. He was mad with rage and despite suffering both pain and a loss of blood, was determined to avenge his brother's death. As he ran, he blazed away one-handed with the rifle, aiming at everything and nothing.

Stone watched the outlaw come towards him in an unsteady, zig-zagging run. He grinned savagely as Judd's bullets either whistled overhead or ricocheted harmlessly off the sides of the ravine. Then, when the outlaw was no more than twenty feet away, the Kentuckian sprang up from behind the boulder and emptied the Winchester into him.

The slugs tore through the elder Judd, smashing through his rib-cage and exiting out of his back in a crimson cloud of blood and bone. The outlaw fell to his knees, coughing up blood and throwing down the now-empty Spencer. His right hand clutched at the butt of his Remington, but, before he could draw it from the holster, Stone's last shot struck him plumb between the eyes and blasted his brains out. He gurgled rather than cried, and slumped forward onto his face.

Behind him in the cottonwoods, Joe Daly swore long and hard. He had anticipated that Jack Stone would prove to be a difficult man to kill. Nevertheless, he had reckoned that, with the odds of five to one in their favour, he and his gang should be more than a match for the Kentuckian. Now, within a couple of minutes, those odds had been reduced to three to one, and Daly was no longer so sure of success. He glanced to his left, to where Bear and Randy Wilkins each crouched behind trees, guns in their hands and their eyes fixed on the mouth of the ravine.

"I don't want no more heroics," he hissed. "Either of you try chargin' at that sonofabitch an' he'll plug you for certain."

"So, what are we to do, Major?" enquired Bear.

"I ain't sure. Did you observe whereabouts Stone's located?" rasped Daly, nervously fingering the sabre cut that decorated his left cheek.

"He's behind that big rock on the left there, jest inside the mouth of the ravine," said Randy Wilkins.

"Hmm." Daly pulled his binoculars from their case and focused on the rock. "We ain't gonna shift him outta there very easily," he commented.

"Mebbe I could crawl across that there scrubland towards him an' . . ." began Bear.

"Nope," said Daly. "Don't even think about it. Stone'd spot you 'fore you got ten yards."

"There's some scrub I could hide behind," protested Bear.

The outlaw chief laughed, a harsh, mirthless laugh.

"The few stunted trees an' bushes that are scattered out there wouldn't hide a chipmunk let alone a giant like you," he said.

"The Major's right," agreed Wilkins. "A frontal attack would be plain suicidal."

"Then, I repeat, what are we to do, Major?" asked Bear.

"I'm thinkin', so shuddup for a minute," retorted Daly.

Silence descended. The three outlaws continued to stare morosely across the scrubland towards the ravine, while Stone used the lull to reload his Winchester. He was beginning to feel that he might, after all, get the better of the outlaws. A bitter wind whistled down the ravine, the kind of wind that, in a few hours, would freeze a man's blood. Therefore, they could not afford to sit it out for too long. Unless they wanted to die of exposure, they would have to make some sort of move.

The same thought had occurred to Joe Daly. Should the situation remain at its present impasse, it was likely that both Amy Scarlett and Jack Stone would freeze to death. But that would scarcely benefit him and his men since they would almost assuredly suffer the same fate. He turned to the others.

"Okay, boys," he said. "This calls for a li'l cunning."

"You gotta plan, then?" asked Bear eagerly.

"Yup. What I aim to do, is to drop back half a mile, an' then work my way round, by way of them bluffs over yonder, to the far side of that there ravine. Then, I'll creep up on Stone from behind."

"What about Miss Scarlett?" demanded Randy Wilkins. "Won't she spot you an' warn Stone?"

"Don't worry, Randy," smiled Daly. "I'll take care of her. Mebbe even use her as a hostage."

"Hell, that's an idea!" exclaimed Bear.

"Yeah. Wa'al, it's gonna take me the best part of an hour, so in the meantime you fellers gotta keep Stone occupied. I don't want him slippin' off. I want him exactly where he is now."

"Sure thing, Major. We'll jest keep pepperin' that ole rock with bullets. He won't be goin' nowhere," grinned Bear.

"If 'n' he tries, it'll be my pleasure to fill him full of holes," added Randy Wilkins.

Daly nodded.

"Okay, start shootin'," he snapped.

His two pardners opened fire and he slowly retreated into the cottonwoods, leading his horse by the bridle. Then, when he reached the far edge of the wood, Daly mounted the chestnut gelding and headed back down the trail, the way he had come.

The detour was necessarily a lengthy one, for Daly had no wish that Stone should spot him. It was a long, cold climb up onto the bluffs and an even longer and colder ride along the ridge to the western end of the ravine. A steep descent followed, one that required all Daly's skills as a horseman.

On reaching the ravine floor, Daly glanced about him. It was here, at the western mouth of the ravine, that the trail split. At this point, Stone would have either continued west to Rock Springs or turned south to Laramie. It didn't much matter now what his plans had been, for Daly was between him and his destination. The Kentuckian would be riding no further. Daly permitted himself a wintry smile and, turning his horse's head, trotted slowly into the ravine.

As he rode cautiously through the ravine, he could hear the shots still being exchanged between Stone and the two outlaws. He took comfort from this. Provided his two confederates kept their heads down, there was no reason why either should be hit, and they could keep the Kentuckian tied down indefinitely. He reckoned the ride had taken him just under an hour, more or less as he had expected. Another five to ten minutes and he would be in a position to give Stone a very nasty shock indeed!

While Joe Daly was cautiously working his way round to the rear of the Kentuckian and Bear and Randy Wilkins were keeping him pegged down, Amy Scarlett was nervously pacing back and forth inside the cave, where Stone had left her. She was shivering with cold, despite the blanket which she had wrapped round herself. And she was consumed with fear. Fear for Jack Stone and fear for herself.

What, she asked herself, should she do? The shots echoing down the ravine told her that a gun-battle was in progress. And, while the shooting continued, she knew that Stone must still be managing to hold out. Should she go to his aid? She continued to hesitate, for she was smart enough to realise that she would probably only get in his way. Although she had carried a Derringer for her protection, she had fired it only once, and that was during the recent hold-up. She had no real experience of handling guns and could prove more of a liability than an asset. Nevertheless, she was anxious to find out what the situation was. Not knowing how the battle was progressing seemed to make matters worse.

The minutes ticked by. Amy continued to debate whether to venture forth or not. The tension slowly built up inside her until she could bear it no longer. She had to know what was happening.

It was unfortunate that Amy chose to leave the safety of the cave at the very moment Joe Daly appeared round a bend in the ravine. She stopped in her tracks on the threshold of the cave. She was transfixed. A look of abject horror wreathed her pale features and she felt suddenly sick.

Daly smiled coldly. He approached the blonde, dismounted and, drawing his Army Model Colt, pointed it at her heart.

"Wa'al, if it ain't Miss Amy Scarlett!" he exclaimed.

"How . . . how d'you know my name?" she quavered.

"A mutual acquaintance told me."

"But . . . but we . . . we ain't got no mutual acquaintances!"

"Oh, yes, we have!" Daly grinned and said quietly, "How's about Marshal John Bannerman?"

Amy gasped. So it was the marshal who had put the Wyoming Phantoms on her trail!

"I . . . I cain't believe that Marshal Bannerman would have . . . would have . . ." She paused, lost for words.

"He was a pretty tough hombre, but me an' the boys, we got him to talk . . . eventually," said Daly.

"You . . . you tortured him!" cried Amy accusingly.

Daly laughed.

"'Course we tortured him," he snarled.

"But why come after me? I was on my way to 'Frisco, where I couldn't possibly be any danger to you."

"Yo're the only person alive who has seen us, the only person who could bear witness against us."

"But . . . but I wouldn't. Truly I wouldn't. Let me go an' I swear . . ."

Again Daly laughed.

"You ain't goin' no place an' neither is yore friend, Stone. This is the end of the trail for both of you," he rasped.

"Okay! Okay! Kill me if you must, but let Jack go. After all, what's he ever done to you?"

"He's shot two of my men."

"Oh!"

"So, c'mon, let's mosey on down this here ravine to where the shootin's at."

"No! Please!"

Amy's protests were cut short, as Daly grabbed her roughly by the arm and jabbed the muzzle of his revolver into the nape of her neck.

"Yo're comin'. An' I warn you, you so much as open yore mouth an' I'll blow yore brains out," snarled the outlaw.

Amy clenched her teeth and permitted Daly to drag her along with him. She was too terrified to struggle. The gun at her head had the effect of coercing her into both silence and submission. She was convinced that she was going to die, yet still she wanted to prolong her life for as long as possible.

As it was, a careless step and the clink of a few loose pebbles alerted the Kentuckian to their presence. He had run out of ammunition for the Winchester and had reverted to using his Colt. Consequently, he spun swiftly round, revolver in hand, to face Joe Daly. And there he crouched, with his gun aimed directly at the desperado's heart.

"Stand up, Stone, an' drop yore gun," said Daly.

"An' if I don't?" retorted Stone.

"Then, I squeeze this here trigger."

Stone stared hard and long at the outlaw. Then, he looked into Amy's terror-stricken features and shrugged his broad shoulders. Slowly, he rose to his full height. And he lowered, but did not drop, his gun.

10

"OKAY, boys, you can come out from among them there trees!" yelled Daly.

Stone glanced over his shoulder and watched the two figures emerge from the cottonwoods. They walked side-by-side across the scrubland, the giant Bear and the slim, black-clad Randy Wilkins. They, too, had abandoned their rifles. Bear clutched a Remington in one of his huge fists, while Randy Wilkins toted his pair of pearl-handled British Tranters. Bear lumbered forward, taking long, ungainly strides, and the youth walked with a cocky swagger to his step, both of them ready and eager to avenge the deaths of the two Judd brothers.

"So, yo're the infamous Wyomin' Phantoms," said Stone contemptuously. Then he glanced at the two corpses and added, "Leastways, what's left of 'em."

"Shuddup," snapped Daly. He stared pointedly at the Colt in Stone's right hand. "I thought I told you to drop that gun," he hissed.

"So you did, but I reckon, if I'm gonna die, I might as well go down fightin'. Reckon on takin' some of you fellers with me, y'see," drawled Stone.

Daly glared at the Kentuckian and jabbed the barrel of his revolver even harder into Amy's neck, causing her to cry out.

"You drop that gun or I blow Miss Scarlett's brains out here an' now," he said.

"Yo're gonna kill her anyways," replied Stone coolly.

"Now, don't git smart, Stone. You wanta see her brains splattered all over the place, you just keep hold of that gun of yourn." Daly's eyes glittered furiously. "I'm gonna count up to three an' then, if 'n' you haven't dropped that gun, I'm gonna squeeze this trigger," he rasped.

Stone glanced from the outlaw leader

to his two pardners, who were now no more than thirty feet away. They stood there, grim-faced, their guns trained on the Kentuckian. Ever the optimist, he reckoned that, if he moved real fast, he might just manage to out-shoot all three and survive. The odds were against him, but there remained a slim chance.

"One!"

On the other hand, to do so would certainly bring about Amy's death. Could he justify sacrificing her life to save his own? Well, she was going to die anyway and ...

"Two!"

The Kentuckian's grip on the Frontier Model Colt slackened. Then, all at once, Randy Wilkins, who had been viewing the Kentuckian with a plainly murderous eye, screamed, threw up his arms and toppled forward onto his face.

In that split second, both Amy and Stone acted.

The unexpected scream naturally

startled all of them. It caused Joe Daly to momentarily relax his grip on Amy's arm, whereupon the blonde ripped herself free from his grasp and threw herself down onto the snow.

As Amy pulled clear of Daly, so Stone raised and fired his gun in a movement quicker than a copperhead's strike. The bullet struck Daly in the chest and knocked him backwards. He hit the ground with a thump and slumped onto his back, where he lay with a great stream of crimson seeping slowly out of a huge hole in the front of his military greatcoat.

Bear, meantime, reacted rather slowly. His first move was to peer down at the prostrate figure of Randy Wilkins. And what he saw filled him with horror. An arrow protruded from between the youth's shoulder-blades. He was caught in two minds. Should he shoot at whoever had fired the arrow, or should he shoot at Stone? In the event, he ended up firing at neither.

Jack Stone, having disposed of Joe

Daly, instantly turned and fired at the giant gunslinger. Two slugs ripped into Bear's massive frame. One struck him in the chest, staving in half a dozen ribs, while the other smashed the bone in his right upper arm. He let loose a great roar of pain, and the Remington slipped from his nerveless fingers.

But he was not beaten yet. Enraged, he pulled out the huge, razor-sharp Bowie knife from the sheath at his waist and, clutching it in his left hand, he charged towards the Kentuckian.

Stone stood his ground and fired. Once . . . twice . . . thrice. All three shots struck the giant in the chest. All three would have killed any normal man. But Bear was no normal man. He kept on coming, and Stone, standing there with an empty revolver in his hand, knew that he was staring death in the face.

Then, suddenly, Bear screamed, just as Randy Wilkins had screamed. And, six feet short of the Kentuckian, he halted, threw up his arms and crashed face downwards in the snow. The ground, so Amy Scarlett reckoned afterwards, shook from the impact.

Stone stared down at the second arrow. It had buried itself in Bear's back and penetrated his black heart. The Kentuckian smiled wryly. Where five shots from his Colt revolver had failed to kill the giant, one Cheyenne arrow had succeeded.

He stared across the stretch of scrubland towards the distant stand of cottonwoods. There, at the edge of the wood, was a lone, buckskin-clad Indian sitting astride his pony. The Cheyenne brave whose life Stone had saved on the previous day. The Cheyenne lowered his bow and raised an arm in greeting. Stone returned the gesture. Then, the Cheyenne turned the head of his coal-black pony and, as silently as he had come, vanished among the trees.

"Wa'al, I'll be jiggered!" gasped Amy, as she struggled to her feet.

Stone smiled, broke open his gun and re-loaded it.

"Guess the Cheyenne must've followed us. Curious to know what we was doin' out here, yet too polite to ask," he said.

"An' then, when he saw our plight, he decided to take a hand," said Amy.

"Yup. I'd saved his life, so he figured on returnin' the favour. Debt of honour, y'see."

"Never thought of Injuns bein' honourable."

"Or polite, as I recall."

"Nope."

"Wa'al, when you git down to it, there ain't all that difference 'tween the white an' the redman. Good an' bad in all of us, I reckon."

So saying, Stone turned and began to check to see if there was any sign of life among the fallen outlaws.

Of the five, only Joe Daly remained conscious, but he was unable to move and was obviously dying. He stared malevolently up at the Kentuckian.

"You bastard!" he hissed. "You . . . you've done for me."

Stone grinned and replied equably, "Yeah. Wa'al, I figure you got yore just deserts, feller."

The two men continued to stare at each other and, as they did so, the expression on Daly's face slowly changed. The malevolence faded and a look of earnest entreaty spread across his pain-wracked features.

"Stone," he gasped, "do me a favour. Finish me off. If 'n' a coyote or a wolf should find me 'fore I die . . . " He left the rest unsaid.

Stone shrugged his shoulders.

"Then, they're welcome to you," he growled, and, turning on his heel, he left the outlaw where he lay.

"Don't you think, Jack . . . ?" began Amy.

"Nope."

"Okay. Wa'al, yo're the boss. So, what now?"

"We gotta choice. Either we retrace our steps to Brough's Ford, where you can pick up the next stage to Laramie, or we ride on. An' I'd better warn you, it's still one helluva ride from here to Laramie."

The blonde smiled happily.

"Oh, we'll press on," she said.

"You sure?"

"I'm sure. We can take it as slow 'n' easy as we like now."

"Okay, then let's go pick up yore hoss."

Leading his bay gelding by the bridle, the Kentuckian walked back up the ravine towards the cave where they had rested overnight. A rejuvenated Amy Scarlett trotted along beside him. Behind them, the scene resembled something of a battlefield. Four dead and one dying outlaw lay in pools of blood that slowly spread across and stained the pure white snow.

"Jack," said Amy, as they walked along, "would you do me one last favour?"

"Name it," replied Stone.

"Stay with me in Laramie till the

train for 'Frisco arrives."

"But you'll be perfectly safe there on yore own."

"Even so."

"It'll cost you. Hotel rooms ain't that cheap an', if I stay, you'll need a couple instead of jest one."

"No, Jack, I'll need only the one."

Stone turned and looked at the blonde. Her wan, forlorn expression had miraculously vanished, to be replaced by one of sheer joy. And he observed her bright blue eyes were twinkling provocatively.

"Amy," he said, "I thought that after yore ordeal you . . . "

"Yeah," she interrupted him. "I couldn't bear the thought of a man even touchin' me, let alone sleepin' with me. But now those sonsofabitch are dead, somehow I feel kinda different 'bout that. An' I'd like you to be the first to make love to me, Jack. If 'n' you'd care to oblige?"

"It'll be a pleasure, Amy," said Stone.

Other titles in the Linford Western Library:

TOP HAND
Wade Everett

The Broken T was big. But no ranch is big enough to let a man hide from himself.

GUN WOLVES OF LOBO BASIN
Lee Floren

The Feud was a blood debt. When Smoke Talbot found the outlaws who gunned down his folks he aimed to nail their hide to the barn door.

SHOTGUN SHARKEY
Marshall Grover

The westbound coach carrying the indomitable Larry and Stretch headed for a shooting showdown.

FIGHTING RAMROD
Charles N. Heckelmann

Most men would have cut their losses, but Frazer counted the bullets in his guns and said he'd soak the range in blood before he'd give up another inch of what was his.

LONE GUN
Eric Allen

Smoke Blackbird had been away too long. The Lequires had seized the Blackbird farm, forcing the Indians and settlers off, and no one seemed willing to fight! He had to fight alone.

THE THIRD RIDER
Barry Cord

Mel Rawlins wasn't going to let anything stand in his way. His father was murdered, his two brothers gone. Now Mel rode for vengeance.

ARIZONA DRIFTERS
W. C. Tuttle

When drifting Dutton and Lonnie Steelman decide to become partners they find that they have a common enemy in the formidable Thurston brothers.

TOMBSTONE
Matt Braun

Wells Fargo paid Luke Starbuck to outgun the silver-thieving stagecoach gang at Tombstone. Before long Luke can see the only thing bearing fruit in this eldorado will be the gallows tree.

HIGH BORDER RIDERS
Lee Floren

Buckshot McKee and Tortilla Joe cut the trail of a border tough who was running Mexican beef into Texas. They stopped the smuggler in his tracks.

BRETT RANDALL, GAMBLER
E. B. Mann

Larry Day had the choice of running away from the law or of assuming a dead man's place. No matter what he decided he was bound to end up dead.

THE GUNSHARP
William R. Cox

The Eggerleys weren't very smart. They trained their sights on Will Carney and Arizona's biggest blood bath began.

THE DEPUTY OF SAN RIANO
Lawrence A. Keating and
Al. P. Nelson

When a man fell dead from his horse, Ed Grant was spotted riding away from the scene. The deputy sheriff rode out after him and came up against everything from gunfire to dynamite.

FARGO: MASSACRE RIVER
John Benteen

The ambushers up ahead had now blocked the road. Fargo's convoy was a jumble, a perfect target for the insurgents' weapons!

SUNDANCE: DEATH IN THE LAVA
John Benteen

The Modoc's captured the wagon train and its cargo of gold. But now the halfbreed they called Sundance was going after it . . .

HARSH RECKONING
Phil Ketchum

Five years of keeping himself alive in a brutal prison had made Brand tough and careless about who he gunned down . . .

FARGO: PANAMA GOLD
John Benteen

With foreign money behind him, Buckner was going to destroy the Panama Canal before it could be completed. Fargo's job was to stop Buckner.

FARGO: THE SHARPSHOOTERS
John Benteen

The Canfield clan, thirty strong were raising hell in Texas. Fargo was tough enough to hold his own against the whole clan.

PISTOL LAW
Paul Evan Lehman

Lance Jones came back to Mustang for just one thing — revenge! Revenge on the people who had him thrown in jail.

HELL RIDERS
Steve Mensing

Wade Walker's kid brother, Duane, was locked up in the Silver City jail facing a rope at dawn. Wade was a ruthless outlaw, but he was smart, and he had vowed to have his brother out of jail before morning!

DESERT OF THE DAMNED
Nelson Nye

The law was after him for the murder of a marshal — a murder he didn't commit. Breen was after him for revenge — and Breen wouldn't stop at anything . . . blackmail, a frameup . . . or murder.

DAY OF THE COMANCHEROS
Steven C. Lawrence

Their very name struck terror into men's hearts — the Comancheros, a savage army of cutthroats who swept across Texas, leaving behind a bloodstained trail of robbery and murder.

SUNDANCE: SILENT ENEMY
John Benteen

A lone crazed Cheyenne was on a personal war path. They needed to pit one man against one crazed Indian. That man was Sundance.

LASSITER
Jack Slade

Lassiter wasn't the kind of man to listen to reason. Cross him once and he'll hold a grudge for years to come — if he let you live that long.

LAST STAGE TO GOMORRAH
Barry Cord

Jeff Carter, tough ex-riverboat gambler, now had himself a horse ranch that kept him free from gunfights and card games. Until Sturvesant of Wells Fargo showed up.

McALLISTER ON THE COMANCHE CROSSING
Matt Chisholm

The Comanche, McAllister owes them a life — and the trail is soaked with the blood of the men who had tried to outrun them before.

QUICK-TRIGGER COUNTRY
Clem Colt

Turkey Red hooked up with Curly Bill Graham's outlaw crew. But wholesale murder was out of Turk's line, so when range war flared he bucked the whole border gang alone ....

CAMPAIGNING
Jim Miller

Ambushed on the Santa Fe trail, Sean Callahan is saved by two Indian strangers. But there'll be more lead and arrows flying before the band join Kit Carson against the Comanches.

GUNSLINGER'S RANGE
Jackson Cole

Three escaped convicts are out for revenge. They won't rest until they put a bullet through the head of the dirty snake who locked them behind bars.

RUSTLER'S TRAIL
Lee Floren

Jim Carlin knew he would have to stand up and fight because he had staked his claim right in the middle of Big Ike Outland's best grass.

THE TRUTH ABOUT SNAKE RIDGE
Marshall Grover

The troubleshooters came to San Cristobal to help the needy. For Larry and Stretch the turmoil began with a brawl and then an ambush.

WOLF DOG RANGE
Lee Floren

Will Ardery would stop at nothing, unless something stopped him first — like a bullet from Pete Manly's gun.

DEVIL'S DINERO
Marshall Grover

Plagued by remorse, a rich old reprobate hired the Texas Troubleshooters to deliver a fortune in greenbacks to each of his victims.

GUNS OF FURY
Ernest Haycox

Dane Starr, alias Dan Smith, wanted to close the door on his past and hang up his guns, but people wouldn't let him.

DONOVAN
Elmer Kelton

Donovan was supposed to be dead. Uncle Joe Vickers had fired off both barrels of a shotgun into the vicious outlaw's face as he was escaping from jail. Now Uncle Joe had been shot — in just the same way.

CODE OF THE GUN
Gordon D. Shirreffs

MacLean came riding home, with saddle tramp written all over him, but sewn in his shirt-lining was an Arizona Ranger's star.

GAMBLER'S GUN LUCK
Brett Austen

Gamblers seldom live long. Parker was a hell of a gambler. It was his life — or his death . . .

ORPHAN'S PREFERRED
Jim Miller

Sean Callahan answers the call of the Pony Express and fights Indians and outlaws to get the mail through.

DAY OF THE BUZZARD
T. V. Olsen

All Val Penmark cared about was getting the men who killed his wife.

THE MANHUNTER
Gordon D. Shirreffs

Lee Kershaw knew that every Rurale in the territory was on the lookout for him. But the offer of $5,000 in gold to find five small pieces of leather was too good to turn down.

RIFLES ON THE RANGE
Lee Floren

Doc Mike and the farmer stood there alone between Smith and Watson. There was this moment of stillness, and then the roar would start. And somebody would die . . .

HARTIGAN
Marshall Grover

Hartigan had come to Cornerstone to die. He chose the time and the place, and Main Street became a battlefield.

SUNDANCE: OVERKILL
John Benteen

When a wealthy banker's daughter was kidnapped by the Cheyenne, he offered Sundance $10,000 to rescue the girl.

RIDE A LONE TRAIL
Gordon D. Shirreffs

The valley was about to explode into open range war. All it needed was the fuse and Ken Macklin was it.

HARD MAN WITH A GUN
Charles N. Heckelmann

After Bob Keegan lost the girl he loved and the ranch he had sweated blood to build, he had nothing left but his guts and his guns but he figured that was enough.

SUNDANCE: IRON MEN
Peter McCurtin

Sundance, assigned to save the railroad from a murder spree, soon came to realise that he'd have to fight fire with fire, bullets with bullets and death with death!